THE SWA[...]

During the long hike from the swamp back to the town of Silverleaf, the men were silent. There was no need to exchange thoughts; they were too similar.

Christopher Dorn, the boy they called the Freak, was running wild and free. His mother, waiting and hoping, would suffer another devastating disappointment.

And Dr. Stefan Vasa, in his determination to study and to dominate, to exploit the power which he had hoped to achieve, had subscribed to the very evil that had twisted and distorted his own life. He had discovered the secret of the swamp—but how long would he live now?

THE SILVERLEAF SYNDROME

Eleanor Robinson

TOWER BOOKS NEW YORK CITY

A TOWER BOOK

Published by

Tower Publications, Inc.
Two Park Avenue
New York, N.Y. 10016

For dearest Ann and John

Prologue

It was almost midnight.

A three-quarter moon cast incandescent light and shadow over the angular lines of their home, perched high over rocky cliffs and sea. The stucco house was studded with unexpected wrought-iron balconies, faded sienna-tiled turrets and surrounded by dense shrubbery and untended beds of flowers.

In his crib in a darkened bedroom on the third floor, the child lay on his stomach, bent knees pulled to his chest, diapered rump elevated. He appeared to be about a year old. His sturdy well-developed body could be indistinctly seen as a narrow swath of moonlight from the half-open door to a balcony crept to the foot of his crib. The back of his head was thickly clustered with pale blond curls. He stirred restlessly when, over the muted sounds of foaming water washing against the tumbled rocks far below and the haunting whisper of a Bach prelude from the stereo downstairs, the heavy thrum of an automobile in low gear could be heard, circling the sharply curving drive to the carport at the back of the house.

The child pushed himself to a crouching position on his hands and knees, listening. A car door slammed and footsteps rapped unevenly on a graveled path. He stood effortlessly and swung his body over the latticed side of his crib, dropping to the floor. A plump ancient poodle, paws clicking on the tiles and tail wagging, snuffled quietly. She thrust up her head for a reassuring pat from the child's blunt strong fingers. Content that nothing unusual was occurring, she returned to her cushioned basket. The child moved into the moonlight at the foot of his crib.

His head was grotesquely enlarged.

Even the well-formed, erect body, naked except for a diaper, with broadening shoulders and muscular arms and legs, could not compensate for the gnome-like imbalance created by his high bulging forehead.

Silently he scampered to his bedroom door, slipped through to the balconied upper hall which led to a winding staircase on the left. Behind the balustrade only the curly top of his huge head was visible as he stood, peering between the ornately carved posts. His dark blue eyes were alive with intelligent curiosity. His face was placid, but intent. In the section of the living room which he could see, his mother lay asleep on a brocaded turquoise couch. She was breathing shallowly, in the fluidly limp position of abject exhaustion. Her right wrist was bandaged.

The outside door to the kitchen slammed. "Claire!"

Dazedly, she pushed up to an elbow. She could have been an unusually attractive young woman. But the thin body in a torn shirt and crumpled jeans, the hollowed darkness circling her eyes in a pallid face and the dark, unkempt hair tumbling around her shoulders made her look ill.

"Claire! Where are you?"

"Here, Gil," she said indistinctly, managing a sitting position.

Behind the balustrade the child held tightly to a carved post as his father, tall and tanned with the same blond curling hair, lurched from the kitchen into the living room. With a crashing thud, he dropped a suitcase and shrugged out of his lightweight plaid wool jacket. He crumped it and threw it across the room.

"Damn good pass. Don't you think?"

Claire stiffened, suddenly, completely awake. "You've been drinking. Again! Gil, you promised—"

"You're goddam right I've been drinking and I'm overdue for another spiritual uplift of sphir. . .sphir. . .oh, hell, another drink. How about you?"

"No, thanks."

His wide shoulder hit the door frame as he staggered back into the kitchen and began shouting over the rattle of ice cubes. "Dad wants me to fly back to Washington in a couple of days. Another bunch of contracts on Survival Kit. That'll be the second damn time this week. Christ! I'm supposed to be a lawyer and I'm nothing but a mesh. . .messenger boy, commuting between L.A. and D.C." The tirade stopped abruptly as if he were gulping a surreptitious swallow.

Claire lay back against the couch. Her face was a pale mask. She closed her eyes, but tears spurted. She rubbed her face hastily and attempted to smooth her hair.

Concealed behind the balustrade, the child crept silently to the top of the stairs where, a half dozen steps down, he sat expectantly, hidden behind a ceramic pot of begonias, now able to see the entire room.

Glass in hand, Gil stomped across the room to the stereo and switched it off. "Sounds like a funeral march."

He dropped to the couch, near Claire. "How about a kiss, Cleo?" He reached for her and she lay against his shoulder briefly. Then pulled away. "Excuse me, Claire!" He drained half the contents of his glass and began a rambling tale of some people he had talked with during his flight. But when he saw she wasn't listening, he broke off. "Okay. Let's have it. How's the baby?"

Claire rubbed at a spot on the knee of her jeans. "I—I took Christopher to another doctor today. An endocrine specialist."

"For God's sake why? That first doctor—what was his name?"

"Dr. Beckstein."

"Beckstein's keeping an eye on him. We're supposed to wait and see what happens. And, so far, nothing much. Nothing much." He drained his glass. "The kid's going to be okay. You'll see. Okay."

Claire shook her head. "But he isn't. I'm with him all the time. Christopher has changed. He's changing all the time."

"So what? A baby has to grow. And grow and grow."

"Gil, listen to me. Just the way Dr. Beckstein wouldn't believe Christopher was only two months old when we first took him, Dr. Marquette wouldn't believe he is only five months old now. All the agility and comprehension tests and physical measurements showed that he could be a year, at least."

Gil averted his face. "He's just a big baby. That's it. Big."

Claire shook her head furiously. "This time I took Christopher's birth certificate from Montana. I suspect the doctor had his secretary call Dr. Vasa in Silverleaf to verify it. And—and I told Dr. Marquette everything. The way Christopher creeps around at night when we're asleep. His toys being moved. About the records, smashed to pieces. The fridge door left open, milk on the floor. And his huge appetite."

"He can put it away. That's for sure. But I still think you're imagining things."

"Gil! You saw what was left of his toy zebra in the garbage compactor!" She shuddered. "Do you think I've been doing all these things?"

He shrugged, examining his empty glass. "I've never seen him do anything. When I'm around, he acts like a fat, funny baby, with a big head and furry skin on his feet."

Huddled on the stairs, Christopher explored the contours of his head and rubbed the soles of his feet with a diminutive frown on his placid face.

"He acts like a baby and when you're around he

10

doesn't do anything because he's protecting himself.'' Claire's voice trembled. ''He knows you don't like him.''

''I suppose he told you that in that mewling whine of his? Christ! Don't start out on my lack of paternal pride, again. He's just a baby and they come in all sizes.''

Claire shivered and clasped her hands tightly. ''Gil, you've got to stop lying to yourself. Christopher has a metabolic imbalance of a growth hormone. He's beginning to show the symptoms. Dr. Marquette is almost certain he has a tumor in the pituitary gland. A tumor in his head at the base of his skull.''

''Say no more. So now it's expensive assays. Tests. And probably surgical resection through the roof of his mouth. So we were told. Right? And the climax. Surgery will drastically affect future growth.'' Gil lurched about the room. ''We can look forward to years of feeding a human vegetable.'' He headed for the kitchen again.

''Don't drink anymore. Please, don't.''

He didn't answer. When he returned his glass was brimming with amber liquid. There was no ice in it.

Claire's shoulders shuddered with repressed sobs. ''The doctor told me that if the tumor is left untreated, it will result in a rare condition. Acromegaly. Gigantism. Exceptional height, enlarged nose, hands, feet. Prominent jaw and teeth. And thickening of his skin. He'll be very strong, at first. And after—after this growing period is over, he will be susceptible to infections. All kinds of diseases. And psychological problems.'' Her voice rose hysterically. ''We can't let that happen!''

Gil began to laugh. ''Maybe it already has. He already looks like a freak. Christopher Dorn, Freak!''

Claire jumped to her feet and stood rigidly. ''And if he does, why! Because we never should have waited

11

the way that first doctor suggested. He should have had those tests three months ago. Three months! It seems like three centuries. Hiding Christopher from everyone, always pretending he has a cold or something. I've made an appointment at that lab in Los Angeles next week to start the tests."

"We can't afford it. You know that. I'll have to ask Dad for help. And he'll learn everything."

"When you fly back to Washington this time, you see that you tell Jasper the truth."

Gil swallowed. His face looked pale as he took her hands. "Honey, listen. You're so upset you're not thinking clearly. Christopher was born full-term, six months after we were married. We told Dad he was premature because if Dad had learned we were sleeping together before marriage, he'd flip."

"I didn't lie to your father. You did. And I—I just went along with you." She was gasping, sobbing. "Why did I do it? God, why?"

"We wanted to protect Dad. Remember? That goddam Digby of the *Times* would have gotten a Pulitzer Prize. Quote, Jasper Dorn, after a lifetime of moral rectitude, has been hung by an umbilical cord, unquote."

She pulled away. "Your father is a hypocritical bigot. Who cares if people sleep together before they're married? And I did it for you. You've always been afraid of him."

"If I am, I have good reason to be." Gil seemed almost sober.

Claire looked at him in cold despair. "You've got to face up to him. To everything. Christopher is horribly ill. And hiding and hoping won't cure him. Look what's happened to us. You drink most of the time. And I don't dare leave the house—" She broke off, thrusting her bandaged wrist behind her back.

Gil blinked and peered. "What happened to your

wrist?'' He jerked at the bandage. The wrist was purple and swollen. Two sets of small regularly spaced teeth marks were visible.

"He bit you!"

"We were playing. He just doesn't realize how strong he is."

Gil stared blindly around the room, then looked down at her with puzzled horror in his eyes. "It's true. Somehow I couldn't—wouldn't believe it. But it's true. Jesus! Our son, a freak. What are we going to do? What can we do?"

"The tests. Christopher is going for the tests. And you will tell your father. He'll have to help us. That's all."

Gil released her so abruptly, she almost fell. "And you know what he'll say? There's nothing in our heritage to account for it. All the Dorn men have been healthy and normal. He'll think our son is an illegitimate bastard. He'll think you were sleeping around with other guys before we were married."

"You can't believe that!"

"I don't know what to believe anymore. But I do know how my father operates. He'll see that Christopher is put away someplace. Out of sight, out of mind. And since you hatched a freak, he'll publicly deplore our divorce but, by God, he'll arrange it."

Claire turned dead-white and swayed. "You're just saying that. You've always been afraid of your father. You're trying to save your own skin."

Gil hurled his glass savagely across the room. It crashed against an impressionist seascape. Picture and glass crashed to the floor. He was breathing hoarsely but when he spoke his voice was venomously calm. "It's time, my darling wife, you heard some very interesting stories. The ugly truth about why my mother died and why Dad's one and only partner committed suicide. And how Dad always managed, at

13

some cost, of course, to save his hypocritical hide."

"I don't want to hear them. Nothing you can tell me will make me change my mind. Christopher goes to that lab next week."

Holding her shoulders, Gil began to shake her. "You're going to listen to it. Every damn word!"

Their voices rose hysterically with Claire trying to twist away and Gil forcing her back on the couch.

Behind the balustrade, Christopher stood and, turning carefully, negotiated the upward step. The poodle, deciding that it was time to investigate, raced toward the child, tail wagging. Her tail hit the pot of begonias. The pot teetered and fell, rolling down the stairs and shattering into shards at the foot.

The young parents were startled into shocked silence. They both looked toward the balustrade in time to catch a glimpse of the boy as he scampered toward his room.

Gil shouted, "The freaky bastard was spying on us! Listening, by God. I've had it!" He raced for the stairs, taking them two at a time.

"Gil!" Claire screamed, running after him. "Gil, don't!"

The child paused in the darkened center of his room, looking about hurriedly. He darted through the door to the balcony and, scurrying around a terrace chair, hid behind a large jade tree, crouching, watching placidly.

The overhead light in his bedroom flashed on. The poodle began to bark furiously.

"Where are you, you little bastard freak?" Gil shouted. He rushed into the closet, searching the shelves, tumbling toys and cartons to the floor. "Come on out, you little monster!"

Claire flew into the room, clutching at Gil's arms. "Stop it! Stop it!"

Gil kicked at the poodle and pushed Claire savagely

14

against the crib when he saw the half-open balcony door. He lurched through it. ''Come on. Come on. Get what's coming to you.''

As he looked about uncertainly in the uneven light, he staggered and tripped over the terrace chair and fell against the balcony railing. The weathered wood held for a moment, then splintered. Screaming hoarsely, he grabbed for a ragged stump of railing and missed. He plunged toward the rocky, foaming surf below.

Trembling, Claire managed to cross the balcony. She fell to her knees and looked down, calling his name. There was no answer. Seagulls rose in a scattered cloud, shrieking raucously. Then she saw the outline of his partially submerged, crumpled figure. She found that she was unable to stand. Panting, whispering incoherently, she inched her body away from the gaping danger of the broken railing.

''Christopher,'' she cried in heightened anguish. ''Where are you? Christopher!''

After a moment, the child emerged from his hiding place with the same placid expression on his face. He crawled toward her on his hands and knees. His massive head made his sturdy body look frail.

Claire took him in her arms and struggled over the floor, inch by inch, into his bedroom. She fell limply against the closed glass doors. Christopher began to pat her face lovingly. His familiar cadenced hoarse mewling was interspersed with barking laughter.

''Don't, don't talk, darling,'' Claire gasped. ''I've got to think what to do. A doctor. The police?'' Her breath caught in her throat. ''And Jasper. I'll have to call Jasper and tell him. Then, he'll know. Oh, my God! He'll know about you. My darling, dearest—'' She cradled Christopher in her arms, crooning and sobbing.

1

(Five Years Later)

Luke Fremont opened a can of beer in the counter kitchen of his studio apartment, head turned to the television across the room which was blasting out the early Friday evening news on KTTV, Los Angeles. The segment had been taped earlier at National Airport in Washington, D.C. A camera panned across the questioning clamor of reporters, TV crews and the curious, crowded around the access gate to the private craft area. Then the camera returned to focus on Jasper Dorn's handsome face with its forcefully sincere expression. He had already answered a half dozen questions about his week's stay in the Capital and his well-known regime of diet and exercise.

It was the performance of a pro, Luke thought with admiration, as he always did. If Dorn announced that the Martians were attacking Washington at midnight, churches wouldn't have standing room. He had probably put in a ten-hour day, making every appointment on his itinerary and he looked now as if he'd had eight hours sleep.

Luke yawned tiredly, shrugged out of his jacket, loosened his tie and flopped down in a leather chair. He sipped and swore. The beer was warm but, in order to reach his apartment and catch the early news, he had been too rushed to search for a thoroughly chilled six-pack.

As editor of the stockholder's report, he synopsized the extensive work done by the research and development departments of Dorn Enterprises, a national octopus of industrial and electronic wizardry. His degrees in science and engineering enabled him to present the esoteric information on a layman's level. But his work was sporadic and elastic and one of his acquired functions was to vet Jasper Dorn's televised appearances for any discrepancy of statement. Not that such an unheard of event had ever occurred. As usual, it seemed that Dorn had everything under control.

He was a tawny lion of a man. Handsome, tall and tanned, with thick greying hair and an athlete's body, radiating poise, geniality and self-assurance. The media and the public loved him. He was photogenic and good copy even though he was an anomaly in an imperfect world, a non-drinking, non-smoking and non-sleeping-around widower, devoted to physical fitness and church on Sundays. In fact, it was this image of impeccable moral standards that, in a time of tottering values and vulnerable men, had captivated the public's adulation.

He raised both arms to quiet the incomprehensible din of voices. "All right. Hold it. I've only got a few minutes." His voice was deeply pitched. "I plan to be on the West Coast a couple of weeks. I have to tend the store once in awhile."

A reporter shouted, "Trouble at the central California plant?"

"Just a foul-up." Dorn elaborated on details of a labor dispute.

Luke frowned. Dorn was making a major issue of a minor situation. And now it seemed that Dorn himself looked tense, troubled.

An attractive newshen shrieked, "The Survival Kit Bill goes to special committee in about a week. You won't be here then?"

"No. Matthew Powell will represent Dorn Enterprises, backed by Senator Farrow. I'm going on to Hawaii for a few days of rest and relaxation."

Shock waves agitated the crowd. Luke was astonished that Dorn wouldn't be around to provide his charismatic persuasion which had resulted in innumerable government contracts. And Survival Kit was perhaps one of the most innovative bills to have ever reached the legislature with Dorn supplying the organizational know-how and Senator Farrow of California, the legislative muscle. Luke knew little about it.

It was a top-secret development of Enterprises. Details had not been released to the media beyond what everyone knew that, short of nuclear war, its contents—food concentrates, vitamin supplements, oxygen, antiseptics, antibiotics—were designed to provide a means of survival in almost every contingency from excessive water and air pollution to fuel and power shortages. And, if it became mandatory for every American to own one, as Farrow intended, the profits would choke a computer.

"Are you disturbed by rumors that the Kit is nothing more than a collection of ordinary home remedies or, even worse, that the Kit contains drugs which will provide some measure of population control?" The questioner was Digby of the Los Angeles *Times* who was an outspoken critic of Dorn's. His more virulent columns always implied that anyone who so avidly projected an image of moral rectitude must have plenty to hide.

Dorn smiled stiffly. "I'm not at all disturbed. We can't foresee all environmental disasters, of course. But the increase in population and dwindling natural resources will become major global problems by the end of this century. The Kit is designed to save life. Its detractors won't. The rumors are malignant and unfounded."

There was a flutter of applause. Then someone asked if he intended taking his daughter-in-law and grandson, Christopher, to Hawaii with him. The tense smile on Dorn's face constricted into a cold frown.

His tawny eyes grew opaque. "I don't answer questions about my family. You all know that's been my policy since Gilbert's death almost five years ago."

"Damn fool question," Luke muttered, feeling a thrust of sympathy. Everyone knew that Dorn still grieved over his son's tragically fatal accident. And it was all the more tragic because it was also common knowledge that Gilbert had rarely been completely sober, although there had been no mention of it in the official investigation.

On the screen Dorn's executive secretary, Matthew Powell, pushed through the access gate, informing his employer that the plane was ready to take off. Like everyone who worked for Dorn, who disliked physical irregularities, he was tall and, in appearance, healthy and reasonably personable. Powell was a black and probably knew as much about Dorn Enterprises as Dorn himself.

Dorn glanced at his watch. He uttered a few fine phrases which, in a less magnetic personality, would have sounded stuffily moralistic. "And God bless you all." Both men disappeared through the access gate to board the private King Air turbojet, cheers accompanying them.

Luke switched off the television. He poured what was left of the can of warm beer in the sink and built a Scotch over ice. He was puzzled. Dorn's elaboration about the labor dispute was certainly out of character. Possibly the lie concealed a personal reason for the unexpected trip to the Coast. But for Dorn to permit personal considerations to interfere when the Survival Kit Bill was going to committee was totally incomprehensible.

Luke decided to call Matthew Powell. He was supposed to anyway if he detected anything off-key in Dorn's public statements. Luke poured another drink and dialed the Dorn Building.

Matthew Powell answered on the first ring. "Fremont, hello. I just got in from L.A. International." There was nothing of the South in his tersely enunciated speech. Powell had graduated from Harvard with honors in business administration.

"I just caught the TV interview at National. I was astonished to hear that Mr. Dorn isn't going to root for the Kit personally."

There was a long pause before Powell said slowly, "I didn't know it either until this morning. I pointed out that Jas was sure to be subpoenaed, if and when the committee decides the rumors have any veracity."

"The rumors are stupid. The Kit hasn't even been tested." All contents of the Kit were scheduled for a vigorous analysis by the Food and Drug Administration.

"Yes, I agree. And Jas said that if the hearings began to stumble, he would appear voluntarily. But if he were there initially, his presence would be of enormous psychological value. It's a devastating concept for the average person to comprehend, that the future of the human race might depend on a glass of unpolluted water or a breath of fresh air."

Luke took a drink of his hopefully unpolluted Scotch. He wished he hadn't called Powell who always made such a point of airing his brains. "I heard today that the Securities and Exchange Commission is getting into the act."

"Yes. In spite of our pyramid of interlocking directorates, subsidiaries and holding companies, since Dorn Enterprises holds all patents and copyrights, the SEC is investigating the possibility that there is a violation of anti-trust laws."

"Investors must be protected. All those widows and orphans."

Powell's voice took on a steely tone. "In addition, the International Trade Organization is concerned about foreign export and its effect on the balance of world trade.''

Luke wondered, and not for the first time, how any man could have the energy and guts to combat such overwhelming complexities. ''Then there must be some damn good reason for Mr. Dorn to cop out. Anything I should know?'' More than once a creative spirit in a research lab had gone into orbit.

''I don't think so. Jas has been edgy all week. But after we landed, he told me to take the limo. He hired a car, explaining that he had a dinner engagement in the Valley.''

And that reminded Luke, he had skipped lunch and was overdue for his usual Friday night veal and spaghetti at Tony's down the block. He contemplated asking Powell, who was a bachelor, to join him and decided against it. Their mutuality of office courtesy always seemed to erode in a more intimate atmosphere.

Powell was explaining in his precise way what he assumed was the reason for Dorn's defection. The conference tomorrow morning of West Coast industrialists who were contemplating production units in Taiwan and Hong Kong with an eye to reduced costs. In fact, Powell was at that moment correlating salient facts and figures.

Luke felt more weary. Professional dedication and diligence was what separated the chiefs from the Indians; people like Dorn and Powell from Luke Fremont.

Powell coughed slightly, always an indication that he was about to deliver a broadside. ''I intended seeing you on Monday about this. But I can speak of it now. During the flight Jas mentioned that you have been looking a bit under par. He wondered if your marital problems have been resolved.''

Luke knew his familiar flush of anger and humiliation but managed to restrain himself from telling Powell that it was nobody's damn business but his own. After all, Powell was only implementing Dorn's policy which demanded a happy, healthy team at the shop. And Dorn had, more than once, shown kindness and understanding of Luke's marital disaster.

"My marital problems are completely resolved. My ex-wife is alive and well and married to a Greek, living on a Greek island."

Powell made an exasperated sound. "Luke, have you been drinking?"

Luke eyed his empty glass. "So what? Has the repeal of Prohibition been repealed?"

Powell responded stiffly. "Perhaps I should restate my question. Have you resolved your own problems caused by your marital difficulties?"

"Matthew, there isn't a more contented divorced man on the entire West Coast."

In a less disapproving way Powell suggested he go out and have a good dinner. The tacit sympathy was worse than his criticism had been. Or was it contempt for an inferior man who has permitted a female to destroy his peace of mind?

"Every Friday night I eat Italian at Tony's. Do you want to know my weekly dining-out routine?"

"I hope you'll feel better in the morning," Powell rasped.

They hung up simultaneously.

Luke poured another drink. He was annoyed with himself for having become annoyed. A contented, divorced man? Who was he kidding? Not Powell, nor Dorn and certainly not himself. If he didn't put a few pounds on his six-three frame and fasten a permanent smile on his gaunt face, he might lose his job. And that would be a financial disaster.

Damn Lori!

He strode about the room. Why did memory continue to torture him? He wasn't the only man in the world whose wife had walked out. And he was living with it, wasn't he? And alone.

He eyed the phone. He should call one of the available gals and pyramid a dinner date into a weekend's diversion. That's all they turned out to be. He decided against it. Instead, he went next door and played three games of pinochle with his elderly neighbor, who always took forever because of her arthritic hands. But it brought a flush of pleasure to her pale cheeks; her grandsons didn't turn up very often. After that, he didn't go to Tony's. He nibbled on some leftover steak he had broiled during the previous week and fell asleep under the soporific effect of a late TV movie.

When the telephone rang, he reached for it groggily, looking at the illuminated face of the electric clock. Almost midnight. He picked up the phone. "Fremont, here."

"Luke, thank God you're home." It was Matthew Powell and his voice sounded distantly hollow. "I tried to call you a half hour ago. Where were you?"

"I was sleeping."

"Sorry I was a bit short with you earlier. How do you feel?"

"Fine. I'll turn off the TV." Yawning, Luke stumbled across the room. He discovered he had a slight headache. What was Powell doing, checking up on him? "What's up?"

"I hope you're free this weekend."

"I've got a golf game on tomorrow. I mean, today."

"Cancel it."

Luke frowned. Powell was often terse but never so rudely abrupt. "Isn't it Saturday?"

Powell was coughing violently and had difficulty speaking. "Luke—I—I don't know how to tell you. It's Jas is dead."

"What!"

"Jasper Dorn has been murdered."

Luke felt like a robot, responding mechanically. "Murdered! Where? When?"

"He was found shortly after ten-thirty by a gardener on the grounds of a nursing home, the Hotel del Sol, in Belden Beach."

"Where the hell is Belden Beach?"

"North of San Luis Obispo, off the old U.S. 1."

"What was he doing there?"

"I don't know. I told you earlier, after we landed, he rented a car and left for a dinner engagement in the San Fernando Valley. That's the last I saw of him."

"How did he die?"

"Shot in the back. Twice at close range. There's a possibility he was mugged and robbed on a beach. His body was covered with sand. It is assumed he was then transported to the nursing home. Federal authorities have been called in. I'm expecting them any minute. Luke, I want you to drive up to Belden Beach, make formal identification and telephone me as soon as you can so I can prepare a statement for the press. But I want you to stay there over the weekend in the event specific information is available. See what develops."

It occurred to Luke that there were a number of men whose seniority would better represent Dorn Enterprises, but the errant thought was lost with Powell's next statement.

"Between us, I think a mugging is unlikely."

"Why?"

"Why didn't his assailant conceal the body in the ocean? Instead he was moved to the grounds of an exclusive nursing home. And there's another reason I think a mugging is not the answer."

"And what's that?"

"You know how fastidious Jas is—was, and his

24

intense dislike of physical imperfection. It has to be someone who knew him well.'' Powell's voice quavered. ''His face is mutilated. Excessively so.''

Luke swallowed. He felt a rising nausea.

''The news of his death hasn't been released to the media yet. So get up there as soon as you can. Ask for John Chang. I believe he's the chief of police. I've already given him your name. He's expecting you.''

Luke's head began to work. ''Have you notified his daughter-in-law?''

''Claire Dorn? No. Her telephone in Palos Verdes has been disconnected. So she and Christopher must have moved. Of course, when she hears about it on the radio or TV, she'll certainly contact me. But I don't like to think of her hearing it that way. Anyway, call me soonest. Tell me everything and anything. No matter what it is.''

''What am I supposed to be looking for?'' Luke asked uneasily.

''I'm not sure. I'll tell you my suspicions later. For now, just eyeball it.'' Powell rang off.

Luke slumped on the edge of the convertible couch. His nausea had lessened but the shocking fact of Jasper Dorn's death had to be absorbed, adapted to the parameters of ordinary life. Luke could vividly recall the news segment, a handsome, energetic man who, although he operated at the apex of power and politics, could be kind and understanding to his associates.

How can you tolerate the frustration, the revulsion and the rage you feel when a man like Dorn falls prey to some miserable mistake of fate?

Luke telephoned his golf partner and cancelled the game. He swallowed two aspirin, took a cold shower and packed a weekend bag. In the subterranean garage of his apartment house, he dug through the glove compartment of his Mustang for a California road guide. Belden Beach wasn't even on the map. Suddenly, he swore. The gas needle hovered on zero. He wasted almost a half hour trying to find a gas station that was still open.

By the time he reached Belden Beach, it was almost four. There was some sort of local celebration going on in the small coastal town, a scattering of stuccoed, tiled stores and homes with a single pier jutting into the dark expanse of the Pacific Ocean. The town was jammed with automobiles, local fishermen, curious tourists and a bearded, blue-jeaned group from a commune. Rock music from a blaring transistor radio completed the rakish carnival scene.

When he asked directions to the police station, he was told that someone had been found murdered up at the nursing home. And then when Luke saw the TV network vans and the cameras, microphones and sound equipment, he knew the news had been leaked to the media that the murdered man was Jasper Dorn.

He was told by a yawning sergeant in the small frame building, the Belden Beach Substation, that Deputy Chang was supervising a search of the grounds at the home. After some difficulty locating it to the north, up in the hills—signs were so discreet as to be non-existent—Luke decided that Powell's description of the home as being exclusive was a masterpiece of understatement. It was practically impenetrable. At the gate house, some distance from the main buildings, under the wary eyes of two uniformed guards, Luke had to produce sufficient identification to permit him, with one of the guards as escort, to enter the lavishly landscaped grounds, skirt the expensive cluster of Swiss chalets and annexes, a glittering swimming pool, tennis courts and recreational areas, to a remote heavily wooded area beneath the intersecting corners of a high stone wall. The area was illuminated by automobile headlights and the flicker of flashlights

26

among the dense trees. Other Hôtel guards watched impassively. The eerie scene looked like a surrealistic movie.

Luke's escort pointed out Deputy Chang who was standing by a black and white squad car and Luke pulled up beside it. The escort departed without a word.

2

Deputy John Chang didn't notice Luke's arrival. Worriedly resentful, he was watching the activity. His disciplined anger wasn't due to the fact that the Monterey county sheriff had usurped his local authority and was in charge of the search. Sheriff Marc Mintner, a hard-faced, laconic man, was acting on orders from federal authorities. But Mintner's brusque indifference to Chang's suggestions had rankled. The search was ineptly organized and should have been delayed until daylight. Watching the erratic flicker of flashlights, Chang was convinced that unless one of the men stumbled across a bloodied knife or a shotgun, which was unlikely, it was more than likely that footprints or the path an inert body leaves when dragged across dusty clay would be obscured.

"Deputy Chang," Luke called out as he left his car. His legs were stiff after the long drive. "I'm Luke Fremont."

Chang turned his wise, thoughtfully curious eyes to Luke. The policeman was surprised. He had expected an older man who would austerely represent a business empire. Instead, he saw a weary and unhappy young man. "From Dorn Enterprises?"

"Yes." Chang's penetrating glance made Luke feel like a schoolboy. He wished Powell had sent someone else.

"Would you mind waiting in your car until they finish?"

Luke stumbled back to the Mustang, sat down tensely and folded his arms, resting his head on the steering wheel.

Sheriff Mintner raised his harsh voice. His heavy body was sagging with fatigue. "Okay, guys, let's

quit for now. Maybe we'll pick it up in the morning."
A moment later he told Chang, "Not a damn thing. A
few footprints. Probably the gardener's."

"Are you going to rope off the area?" Chang asked.

"Stop bugging me," Mintner said angrily.

Obviously he had given orders to rope off the area.
A perimeter of trees formed a natural barricade and
the ropes were secured in a short time. The searchers
departed in their escorted automobiles, restoring the
area to faint starlight and deep shadow.

Chang walked over to Luke's car. His slim, erect
posture made him look much younger and taller than
he was. He pulled off his visored cap and rubbed his
head vigorously. His face was unlined but the dark
sleek hair was tempered with grey. "Murder has no
consideration for the eight-hour working day."

"I was thinking the same thing. But Matthew Powell asked me to make identification. Where. . .is the
body?"

"Up at the Hôtel." Chang pronounced the word
with a French accent, without the 'h' sound. "We
moved him to the morgue there because we don't have
one in town. You'd better come along with me and
I can report to the director, Mr. L. Avery Boyd. I
never could decide whether the L stood for limp or
lonely."

The irrelevant observation made Luke feel less
tense.

"There's one other thing," Chang said. "On orders
from the county coroner's office, Mr. Dorn's body is
being moved to Los Angeles for autopsy so he is just
as we found him, dressed, and no medical examination
has been made beyond assuming that the two bullet
wounds must have been the cause of death."

Luke followed the squad car. At the main lodge,
wide glass doors, artfully reinforced with a floral pattern in filigreed iron, were locked. Chang pushed a

soundless bell. "The security system here is supposed to be better than best."

A white-jacketed orderly stood behind the doors as they recessed electronically and the orderly swiftly ushered Luke and Chang through the wide green and gold foyer, past a series of alcoves luxuriously draped and carpeted and furnished with low cushioned chairs, convenient tables, tall lamps and large urns of potted foliage. The overall impression was that of an expensive, exclusive spa.

The men had reached a maze of antiseptically shining corridors and entered a small, frigidly cold room. Its only occupant was a motionless white-swathed figure on a narrow table. The orderly raised the sheet.

It was the moment Luke had been dreading and it turned out to be worse than he had anticipated. The mutilated face was unrecognizable, but the heavily greying hair was unmistakably Dorn's. And the lightweight grey plaid suit, although sodden with sand, was the one seen earlier on the TV news. His chronometric watch was missing but the wide gold wedding band he had always worn, although widowed for two decades, encircled a finger, obviously swollen as if his assailant had tried and had failed to remove it.

"Yes," Luke said in a low voice. "It's Jasper Dorn." He turned away quickly but the featureless face seemed seared in his memory. It transformed what had seemed a senseless act of brutality into one of obscene degradation. Powell's surmise that Dorn's death was not the result of a mugging, but a murder, conceived in hate and vengefully executed, seemed a certainty. Luke closed his eyes and felt Chang's hand grip his elbow. Suddenly they were back in the luxurious foyer again.

The orderly disappeared and an older woman, grey hair piled elegantly, wearing a green pants suit, greeted them. She was carrying a small tray which she placed

30

on a low table. "Chang, how nice to see you again. How is your niece?"

Chang laughed. "Still practicing her English." He took her hand and introduced Luke who found, now that the ordeal was over, reaction had set in. He felt ready to drop.

She looked at him sympathetically. "I thought you might need coffee. And a brandy. Avery will be with you shortly."

Chang thanked her and, when she left, told Luke that Hilda Beck was the only sane and sensible person in the place. "Boyd is her brother."

Luke closed his eyes again and Chang forced a glass in his hand.

L. Avery Boyd entered the room so swiftly and silently he might have materialized in front of them. He was tall and spare, limp dark hair swept severely back from a broad, pallid forehead. Hands in the pockets of a dark blue, faultlessly tailored suit, he acknowledged the introduction with an affected nod and the obsequious manner of an undertaker greeting the bereaved family.

Chang told him that the body had been positively identified.

"The identification was ascertained earlier, I believe." Boyd spoke extremely rapidly, breaking the rhythm of his sentences at odd intervals. "The itinerary of his recent trip to Washington, which his assailant overlooked, was found in a jacket pocket."

"Yes, well," Chang cleared his throat, "there's no evidence that the murder took place on the grounds, although there may be another search during daylight hours. There are no signs of a struggle and only an acceptable amount of terminal bleeding. It would seem that Mr. Dorn must have been killed someplace else."

"Of course," Boyd commented nervously. "From the moment my gardener discovered the body which

31

was innundated with sand. There is no sandy soil on the grounds. I pointed that out. At the time.''

"So you did," Chang said politely. "And I pointed out that Mr. Dorn was a large, heavy man. The assailant, to have lifted his inert body over the high wall and to have carried him, not dragged him, to that remote area would have needed near superhuman strength. Still, that's what must have happened. My office has been informed that federal authorities are moving the body to L.A. for autopsy and are taking over the investigation." He glanced at his watch. "They should arrive any minute now. Will you inform your guards at the gate?"

"Of course. Now, if you'll excuse me—"

"Just a minute," Chang said hurriedly. "There's another problem. Belden Beach is crowded with reporters and TV people asking for permission to film the area where Mr. Dorn was found. They also want to interview you and the gardener."

"I have anticipated that possibility. I absolutely refuse. No one will be permitted on the grounds. And there will be no interviews with me or my employees. The Hôtel is a nursing home, not a circus. My patients are people who require physical and mental peace. And, above all, privacy."

Chang seemed to be having such a rough time, Luke broke in persuasively, ignoring Chang's surprised glance. "I agree with you, Mr. Boyd. But I wonder if you might give me some information. The police are in charge but Mr. Dorn's murder will have an adverse impact in many areas, particularly the Survival Kit legislation."

Boyd, who was already halfway across the room, turned. "Of course. Naturally."

The corners of Chang's mouth twitched as he restrained a smile. Luke was pretending sympathy in order to induce Boyd to be a bit more cooperative.

"If there is anything you can tell me, even your suspicions, I would certainly appreciate it. It would be off the record, of course."

Boyd returned and suggested they sit down. In a few minutes he had set the record so straight, there wasn't any record left. No, he didn't know Jasper Dorn. He knew of him, of course. The reasons for his body being found at the nursing home were unknown to him. Possibly it was the result of another pointless act of violence. The gardener, Sprague, an old and trusted employee, had been checking traps he had set for coyotes which were terrorizing patients with their howling at night and had inadvertently stumbled across the body. And absolutely not. Dorn had no relative or friend in the Hôtel.

"I wonder if I might see a list of the patients' names? There might be a relationship you were unaware of."

"That is impossible." Boyd stood abruptly. "Every patient is identified by number and none of the staff knows identities. Correlating records are coded on microfilm and kept under lock and key in my office files."

Chang frowned. "There was a leak in your private bathroom one night and your office was flooded. An orderly—what was his name?—Groder, discovered it and in the confusion a great many people had access to your office."

Boyd looked away uneasily. "There was nothing missing in the files. I checked them very carefully."

Chang sighed, and picked up his visored cap. "You will undoubtedly be required to answer these questions and others by federal authorities."

"But I've already talked with Sheriff Mintner." Apparently further questioning was not a possibility that had occurred to Boyd. Wrinkles of displeasure creased his broad forehead as he led the way to the front entrance. "Scores of people knew Mr. Dorn.

And certainly a man with his power and money, must have had many enemies. Jas was no—''

Luke, who was a step behind the two men, missed a step. ''What did you say?'' And he instantly regretted it.

Boyd faltered, then said smoothly, ''I was saying that I imagine Jasper Dorn was not a man one knew on a personal level. He compelled admiration. But he was so highly motivated and possessed tremendous vitality. He was a public figure in every sense of the word and he probably never gave a thought to the mundane considerations of friendship and social intercourse. This is all supposition, of course.''

The doors behind Luke and Chang hissed smoothly and closed with a faint click.

''Limp or lonely?'' Chang asked.

''Both. And that is a bunch of bull. Didn't you hear what he said?''

''It seemed a thumbnail psychoanalysis of Dorn's personality.''

''No. Boyd called Dorn, Jas. I've heard only two men use that nickname. Matthew Powell and Senator Farrow. I think Boyd is lying. He must have known him.''

''It's possible,'' Chang said thoughtfully.

Luke reserved the coincidence for future thinking.

They looked up at the sky. Dawn was due any minute. A misty fog blanketed the Hôtel del Sol and its wooded grounds. The effect it created was ghostily secretive. At intervals a far-off bell buoy tolled mournfully.

''Are you going back to Los Angeles now?'' Chang asked.

''God, no.''

''Then why don't you follow me back to the beach? I should check on how much mischief that crowd was up to during the night and I'll steer you to one of the motels.''

34

As Luke trailed the squad car into town, an ambulance and three sleek dark sedans passed them swiftly, headed toward the Hôtel, federal authorities arriving to put official wheels into action.

Belden Beach seemed deserted. The carnival fever had blazed briefly and had died. Beyond a number of broken windows in the store fronts along Beach Road and beer cans littering the sidewalks, the damage seemed to be minimal, until the squad car reached a small appliance store and drew to the curb. Luke pulled up behind it.

The proprietor, a paunchy man wearing a sweater yanked over pajamas, was trying to fit some ragged ends of boards over the broken front window. When he saw Chang, he exploded.

"Damn it, why weren't you in town last night?"

"I was on stand-by duty up at the Hôtel, Mr. Mobley."

Mobley dropped a board and swore. "My wife and I heard the crash and there he was, one of those longhairs from the commune. He lifted out a radio as cool as you please."

"And a camera!" Mrs. Mobley added, standing in the doorway in a bathrobe.

"Do you want to make a formal complaint?" Chang asked.

"God, no! What good does it do? Just try and get the merchandise back. It's worth a hundred or so." Mobley examined the makeshift barricade. "Jesus!" he said and slammed the door in Chang's face.

"Thanks," Luke called out from his car. "I'll find a motel."

Chang shook his head and continued on toward the beach. It turned out that all three of the motels were fully occupied. Automobiles and network vans and station wagons jammed the parking lots. After a futile inquiry at the third, Chang suggested that Luke bunk down for a few hours at his home. Luke accepted instantly. He was so tired, he could have slept standing up.

Chang toed an empty beer can into the gutter. "I guess I'll miss my early morning swim. The cameras have to film someone for the evening news." He grinned and it made him look 20 years younger. "This will be my first, and probably last, appearance on the tube. Which is my best profile?"

Luke had to laugh. You couldn't help liking this reflective and gently humorous man. "I'll come along and provide moral support, if you like."

"You'd better stay out of the picture. You'll be hounded to death as an employee of Dorn Enterprises. They'll be hoping to uncover pay dirt."

Luke felt hopeful. Since Powell had asked him to look around and see what he might learn, perhaps Chang knew that there was pay dirt to uncover.

Chang's home was the inevitable tiled stucco, but it was imaginatively decorated, inside and out, with unusual plants and trees. Horticulture was a hobby of his, he confessed. In fact, he had converted the garage in the back into a greenhouse.

A slim girl—she couldn't have been more than 17 or 18—greeted them at the door in an ankle-length, sleeveless dress. Her sleek black hair and the yellow gown fell in unswervingly straight lines. There was a fragrance and freshness about her and the smooth faultless skin and dark eyes.

"This is Jade. Her Chinese name is *Jun* which means soft as the dew," Chang explained. "She is one of my many nieces from Hong Kong who is staying with me to perfect her English before she begins her nurse's training at UCLA. She is also a very good cook."

She extended a slim cool hand. "I am preparing breakfast. Ham and eggs, American style. And some jackflaps."

36

"Flapjacks," Chang smiled.

Luke apologized for having appeared at such an inconvenient hour. He hoped it wasn't an imposition.

"Imposition?" Jade turned to her uncle.

"Out of place, I guess."

"Place! Kitchen!" Jade wailed and fled. There was a clatter of pans. The men sat down wearily.

"My other pastime is helping my nieces and nephews to emigrate to the United States where they can pursue more rewarding lives. The only trouble is that my family in Hong Kong grows more rapidly than my resources do. However, Jade's trip was possible this year because I supervised the planting of some of the gardens up at the Hôtel."

"What sort of people. . .patients stay there?"

Chang tapped his forehead with a finger. "A nursing home implies care of the sick and elderly. But the Hôtel is far out of that league. Say you have a substantial bank account and a relative or friend who is a nuisance. Sex, drugs, alcohol. Psychological problems. For a healthy fee you can arrange for him to live luxuriously in one of the front suites or, if he becomes too difficult, much less luxuriously in the back annex, small cells under physical restraint. The patients get the best of medical care on a consultant basis. But, in most cases, there's no hope of a cure. They are kept reasonably content and quiet. Sometimes we see one of them in town, always with a male nurse. Quiet, well-behaved. They're tranquillized out of their heads, I expect."

"No wonder Boyd seems strung out," Luke commented. "Some job."

"Someone has to do it."

Jade announced breakfast.

At the kitchen table she served fried eggs, broiled ham, toasted slices of home baked bread and hot brewed coffee with flapjacks for dessert. Luke concentrated on the food which was decidedly satisfying. Later, he was shown to a largish room, which had been converted into a study. Books on horticulture, science, psychology and philosophy lined one wall behind a somewhat battered desk. Yawning, he stretched out on a studio couch. He intended telephoning Powell around ten, which was less than four hours away. But he slept until after one.

When he awoke, the house was deserted. He found a typewritten note on the kitchen table. Early that morning, the Belden Beach substation had received a call from Matthew Powell. He would be in Los Angeles most of the day at police headquarters. He had already been informed of the details of Dorn's death and had issued a statement to the press. And he would expect a call from Luke around five that evening. Chang had scribbled at the bottom of the page. "Before you leave, drop by the station. Have latest newspapers and official reports."

Luke decided to walk to the station. His legs were still stiff from the drive the night before. Outside, the early morning mist had intensified. Like a blanket of clammy wet smoke, it distorted vision and deadened sound. At the station a young, uniformed woman was manning—or what would be the proper word?—the entry desk and informed him that Chang had just left for the old fishing sloop, moored at the end of the pier.

The six blocks walk was not invigorating. Luke's footsteps echoed hollowly on the deserted streets. He wondered if the air of desertion was typical or just a Saturday occurrence. The air was unpleasantly heavy, an unwholesome combination of the odors of seaweed and fish. As he passed the motels, he saw that the unexpected deluge of overnight guests had receded. The parking lots were virtually empty and the network vans were gone. The reporters and TV people must now be haunting the county coroner's office or police headquarters in Los Angeles.

The shore tide rose and fell sluggishly beneath the pier. The water looked oily and grey. The fishing sloop which had once been a pristine white was yellowed and peeling; its registered name, *Sea Lion,* could scarcely be seen. The sloop listed sharply to the sea side and the hull on the pier side, which was partially exposed, was covered with barnacles and semi-transparent sea life.

"Chang?"

At that moment Chang emerged through the hatchway. He was followed by a half dozen barefoot boys and girls in jeans and T-shirts. Two noisy tail-thumping hounds nosed about the listing deck.

Chang said severely, "This is your second offense this summer. All of you kids know that it is against the law to play on this boat. And it's dangerous. If I catch you here again, I'll report it to your parents. But not at home, like before. At the station where the jail is. Do you understand?"

Their sheepish nods couldn't have been more energetically sincere and they scampered on the pier toward shore, the hounds barking furiously. The men followed slowly.

"They'll be back," Chang said. "It's a crime, leaving this derelict here. It should be towed away for scrap or maybe just sunk and let it pollute the Pacific Ocean."

"Who owns it?"

"A Leo Stone did. Around six months ago, the engines exploded about ten miles off-shore. The Coast Guard found it and towed it back here. Leo's body—or what was left of it after the sharks—was found a week later washed up on a beach to the north."

"Why doesn't the town do away with it?"

"No one can touch it. Leo's brother in Indiana is

39

the legal owner now. The trouble is, he's never turned up and the moorage fees are paid up until the end of the year. Say, come to think of it, I got most of what I know about the Hôtel from Leo who heard all kinds of lurid tales from his friend Broder.''

. ''The orderly who discovered the leak in Boyd's bathroom?''

''Yes.''

''Where could I get in touch with him?''

''You can't. He's dead, too.''

Luke exploded. ''The mortality rate in Belden Beach is damned high.''

''Isn't it everywhere? Groder was found dead, mugged on the beach. Stone came to me in a rage. He was an enormous guy, a loner, and Groder was his only friend. He said Groder would never have walked on the beach at night. He hated the water and he was a coward. And since Groder tended to be. . .well, sadistic in his treatment of the Hôtel clientele, Stone was sure one of the patients had killed him. Why are you so interested in the Hôtel?''

''Boyd's slip of the tongue, using Dorn's familiar name. And Matthew Powell is worried,'' Luke explained. ''He asked me to look around, see what I could pick up. I'd sure like to have a tour of the nursing home.''

''Listen, Fremont. It isn't any of your business and it isn't any of mine. The massive forces of the federal government are doing all the leg work and the thinking. I can appreciate the fact that Powell is worried. There's bound to be some mud slinging. For that matter, you look as if something has been bothering you for a long time.''

''What's bothering me is my own business,'' Luke said angrily.

''Calm down. All I'm telling you is just don't go super-sleuthing around.''

"How could I, Chief? I'm not even an amateur."

Chang replied somberly. "And I'm not a police chief. The last one retired the first of the year. So I inherited the town, but not the title. Since I'm approaching the age of retirement, the county is probably looking for a younger replacement."

They crossed the street in silence. When they reached the far sidewalk, they both began to speak at once. Then they both grinned. "You've got the floor, Luke," Chang said.

"Okay. Powell doesn't think a mugging was the cause of Dorn's death. So I'm asking you, what do you think?"

Chang squinted thoughtfully. "No, it doesn't seem possible, even taking robbery into account. Why did the killer have a knife handy when he intended to use a gun?"

"You mean the mutilation of his face would indicate a personal motive?"

Chang nodded. "And why not conceal the body in the ocean? Why was it taken up to the Hôtel grounds?"

"To draw attention to the Hôtel."

Chang nodded again. "And do you know anyone who could have lifted Dorn over that wall and carried him?"

"Not offhand."

"If Leo Stone were alive, I'd turn him over to the LAPD. He had a motive and he was certainly large and strong enough." Chang shrugged his shoulders.

They had reached the police station. "But I think I'll take a run out to the commune this afternoon. Check on the camera and the radio. And there may be some new talent out there. Want to come along?"

"No. I'm going to try to see Boyd again."

"You can't. He's going to be in L.A. all day at police headquarters for further questioning."

The men exchanged sardonic grins.

In Chang's office Luke studied the slim pile of official reports and scanned the local newspaper and the Los Angeles *Times*. Most of the information was biographical since details were so meager. All the papers carried reprints of the same photograph, Jasper Dorn holding his infant grandson with Claire and Gilbert Dorn to the left of them.

"I wonder if Claire Dorn has contacted the police," Luke said.

"Not yet. I asked Sheriff Mintner to let me know if she had. It seems strange that a young woman whose son will probably inherit a great deal of money has apparently vanished."

And what's more, Luke suddenly realized, she hadn't been around the Dorn Building in some time. He tried to recall if he had seen her since Gilbert Dorn had plunged to his death. "She lives in Palos Verdes. Or did. No one seems to know. Dorn rarely talked about his family."

"What kind of man was Dorn, anyway?"

Luke frowned. "He had so much going for him in a public way. You just assumed he was what he projected."

"How did you get the job with Dorn Enterprises?"

"As a result of an interview just before I graduated from Michigan State."

"It was a great opportunity."

"I thought so at the time." Luke added bitterly, "I was married then." He stood and stretched his long arms. His legs felt less stiff. "All right, Chang. I'll stand you to lunch. Then we'll go to the commune. What do you expect to find?"

"I don't expect anything but 'a journey of a thousand *li* begins at one's feet.'"

"My God, a philosophical policeman."

Chang shook his head. "That quote is from Laotse's *Book of Tao,* written over 2500 years ago. Laotse was

42

quite a guy. He advised *wu-wei*, non-interference. And humility, quietude and calm.''

''Some philosophy for the twenty-first century.''

''We'd better not pursue the subject. It might take all day. And Jade usually has dinner ready at seven.''

Luke felt like a damn fool. He should have packed his things and moved to one of the motels. ''Why don't I take you and Jade out somewhere for dinner?''

''And miss seeing me on the seven o'clock news?''

''I forgot to ask. How was your performance before the cameras this morning?''

''Solemn, dignified. And, if re-takes mean anything, singularly lacking in star quality.''

3

The commune was located some twenty miles inland over a rough dirt road, hardly more than a rutted track. Chang usually drove out once a month, wearing his gardening clothes and driving the old Ford pickup he used to transport plants to his cousin's garden shop in Los Angeles. He fancied that the unofficial visits had given him some degree of acceptance by the commune's fluctuating population. On the way he explained to Luke that the commune was harmless enough, but more than once had unwittingly given refuge to undesirables, like the Red Army factions who were kidnapping and killing wealthy industrialists.

"And you think one of them is responsible for Dorn's death?"

"Could be. Except that there wasn't a demand for money. But it could be part of larger plot."

Luke felt a throb of apprehension. A plot involving the mysterious disappearance of Claire Dorn and her son? His appreciation of Chang's abilities widened. Luke began to study Chang curiously and finally asked him about his background.

Chang laughed. "You mean, how I ended up as a retiring policeman in Belden Beach? It's a good question. I sometimes wonder how and why myself." But he willingly told his story.

He had been born in San Francisco, the only child of parents who had emigrated to America some years before the 1924 immigration act was passed which excluded all Asiatics. He had never been to China but he well knew his family history, impoverished life in reed huts where survival depended on rice and the daily catch of fish. Some of his early forebears had first come to the United States to work on the continental railroads, but Chang was the first of his family to graduate from college.

"I realized that much of human tragedy is caused by people disobeying the ancient and modern laws governing human behavior. So I went into law enforcement. I saw that education is vital if we are to survive as a species."

In 1943, when the Asiatic exclusion act was repealed and the quota system of immigration had been established, Chang, unmarried, had begun to devote his resources sponsoring young members of his family to come to America and acquire an education. And now the focus of a lifetime was rapidly coming to an end.

Chang sighed. "Unless I can find a way to implement my income." He slowed the pickup and parked by a number of dune buggies. "Here we are."

As the men got out of the truck, Luke uttered a surprised sound. Some miles back the coastal fog had dissipated and, in the brilliant sunlight, the huddle of huts looked unattractively squalid.

Chang saw Luke's reaction and laughed. "It always makes me think of sampans moored like beached sardines around a rent-free stretch of shore. I won't identify you and you'd better let me do the talking. They're a trifle touchy about outside interference."

Several young people, dressed in shabby faded clothing, were moving about the center of the settlement, a scattering of wooden benches around an outdoor kitchen. Something was roasting on the hand-operated spit. Chang sniffed. "Wild turkey." He looked about for Lily who was a fairly permanent resident because her husband always seemed to be ill. He saw her approaching the truck. She was a remarkably thin girl, wearing her usual long crumpled and muddied dark skirt and faded halter top. Her long pale hair was wound to a topknot. The flesh of her bony face was pulled taut.

"Lily, hello."

45

She didn't look particularly pleased to see Chang. "Hi." She eyed Luke suspiciously.

"How's your husband today?" Chang asked.

She frowned. "Bud's had trouble breathing. For a week now."

Chang made sympathetic sounds although he privately believed that if Bud could summon half the energy and drive that Lily had, there wouldn't be a thing wrong with him.

"This is Luke," Chang said.

Lily didn't respond to Luke's greeting.

"Is Eric around?" Chang asked. Eric was the idealistic leader of the group, as Luke later learned. He was a slender young man, usually dressed in a contemporary version of a monk's robe. Chang respected his teachings which advocated non-agression and non-violence. But the unfortunate aspect was that, like most revolutionaries, he had not conceived of any workable system that would replace the establishment, once it was overthrown. A house will collapse if its foundation is torn away.

"No," Lily said. "Eric is in Barstow visiting his sick mother."

"Any new members?" Chang asked. Luke thought everyone looked as if they needed a square meal.

Lily shrugged. "Some. Why?"

"There's been a murder at the Hôtel del Sol in Belden Beach."

"Oh, sure. That industrialist, Jasper Dorn. The L.A. police have already questioned everyone out here. He sowed the seeds of his own destruction," she said pompously. "Power. Greed. We held a ritual for the dead this morning." She looked at Chang severely. "You shouldn't be wasting your time this way at your age. A policeman, still persecuting the innocent and protecting the guilty."

Luke stifled a laugh.

Chang ignored her reference to his age. "I'm not connected with the investigation. I brought you something." He pointed to a pile of gunny sacks in the back of the truck.

Lily darted forward and found the bunch of bananas. She smiled and, without her severe expression, she looked almost pretty. "Bud loves them. I'll take him one right now." She disappeared into one of the hovels. Bud's querulous voice could be heard. Lily was probably even peeling the banana for him. She returned shortly. "Thank you, Chang. We do have a problem with fresh fruit and—"

Abruptly a belligerent voice bellowed, "Lily, why is Chang here?" The voice belonged to Kelso who was in charge when Eric was absent. In personality and character he was brute mean, a permanent expression of frowning hostility on his face, brows slashing across a furrowed forehead. He ignored Luke.

Lily looked tensely wary as she jerked at her halter top which was slipping down over her thin breasts, but not before Chang and Luke had glimpsed a livid scar across her bony chest.

"I said, what are you snooping around here for, Chang?"

"Mr. Mobley at the appliance store is missing a camera and a radio."

Kelso sneered. "And they're right over there." He pointed to a long table. "I caught the guy who did it. So now you can leave."

Lily spoke up defiantly. "Chang brought some bananas for Bud."

Kelso hooted nastily. "So now it's bribes. See that they're shared equally among everyone. Got that, Lily?" He swaggered toward the spit, examining the singed fowl.

Lily's fingers massaged her chest gently. "I don't know why Eric keeps him around," she said in a low furious voice. "He told me the other day if Bud couldn't work for his food, he shouldn't be given any."

"I'm sure you do enough work for two people, Lily," Chang said sincerely. "And that makes up for Bud's inability to contribute. I didn't bring the bananas to bribe you."

"I know you didn't."

"Good. I felt you should be told that the county health department turned up last week to fumigate that tub at the end of the pier. An inspection for health violations out here is scheduled for next week. Has Bud seen a doctor?"

"Yes. Well, sometime ago. He was anemic. That's all."

"If it should be anything more serious, he might be taken to the county hospital."

"They'd take Bud away from me!" Her maternal pride flared.

"It would be for his own good."

"What kind of a country is this, anyway?" she said in a shrill voice. "You don't even have the freedom to be sick."

Kelso swaggered back to them. "Now, what's going on?"

At that moment a hoarse voice screamed, "Let me out of here! Let me out!" It seemed to come from a windowless hut on the other side of the clearing.

"That bastard," Kelso said in a low voice.

Chang asked, "Who is it? What's going on here?"

"Maybe Kelso better explain," Lily said with sly triumph.

"Just a guy. He's being punished. He's the guy who took the radio and the camera."

"Let me out, you crud." The howling and sobbing continued.

"Kelso, let him out," Chang demanded.

48

"Listen, the beach is off-limits to us so you're off-limits here. Get it?"

Luke could remain silent no longer. "If you don't, Chang will return with a search warrant. You must be holding him against his will."

Spouting a pungency of obscenities, Kelso stamped across the lot and jerked open the door of the windowless hut which wasn't much larger than a walk-in closet. An odor of excrement hung in the air. A thin young man with long tangled hair and a beard lay on the floor. He was manacled with enough hardware, chains and locks to restrain an elephant.

"Release him," Chang said angrily.

"Jesus," Kelso snarled. But he pulled a ring of keys from his pocket. The captive cowered as Kelso bent over him and, free of the chains, he staggered when he attempted to stand.

By now they were ringed by members of the commune, all ominously silent. Luke couldn't decide whether the group was relieved to see the boy free or were they hostilely resenting Chang's display of authority?

"What's your name?" Chang asked.

"Perins. Jim Perins."

"I can give you a room for a couple of nights at the jail."

"I'm not a vagrant," the youth sobbed. He pulled off a shoe and waved a crumpled money order. It was made out for two hundred dollars.

"Holding out on us," Kelso howled.

"And there's my wheels over there," the boy said. "I'm taking off right now." He brushed at his soiled, stained trousers and moved unsteadily toward his shabby car.

"That crummy little bastard," Kelso said unemotionally. "Go on," he shouted at the others, "get back to work."

49

"How long has this hut been here," Chang asked.

"A year or so," Lily said, "and—"

"Shut up," Kelso told her.

"I'm ordering you to have the hut torn down, Kelso, and all those instruments of torture junked. Get it?" Chang walked over to the table and picked up the camera and the radio.

"And right away," Lily piped up. "The sanitation guys are coming out next week."

Chang returned. "And I'll inform them what to look for. If it isn't gone, you'll be a guest of the county, Kelso, for as long as I can make it stick."

Muttering, Kelso walked away.

Luke asked, "Lily, who thought up that cell in the first place?"

She jerked her head toward Kelso. "He did."

"But why?"

Her face looked as if a wet towel had wiped away all expression. "I don't know. It seems there was someone here once who made a lot of trouble."

She was lying, Luke was certain. But there was no way to pursue it. The men walked back to the pickup and, as they chugged away, Lily waved, a pathetically resolute figure.

"Tribal justice," Luke said.

"It's tribal. But I don't know about the justice. Anyway we found the camera and the radio. And maybe something will come of our visit."

"What do you mean?"

Chang swerved the pickup to avoid a deep rut in the road. He admitted that he was ashamed of his strategy. The bananas had not been a bribe. But the warning that county officials might move Bud to a hospital had been. Lily would undoubtedly spirit her husband away while the inspectors were there. But she would feel obligated to return the favor which would be information about the commune. Lily had her own stand-

ards of honesty which weren't as original as she
believed.

It was after five when they arrived in Belden Beach.
Chang telephoned the substation. The place where
Dorn had been killed had been found. A lonely cove,
near the Costa Marina, south of Belden Beach. The
killer hadn't attempted to conceal evidence of the
struggle or the blood. L. Avery Boyd had been completely cleared of any involvement, although a search
of his files was under way.

Luke's telephone call to Matthew Powell elicited
the information that Claire Dorn had not yet shown
up. Luke agreed to drive to Palos Verdes the next day
and investigate. Then he drove off to the liquor store
to buy a bottle of wine for dinner.

Chang went into the garden to do a bit of weeding.
Crouched on his knees, he reflected that it was serenely
pleasing to work with the rich soil of the earth and not
the dirt of the earth's inhabitants.

Neither man noticed a small brown van which was
parked around the corner.

4

That night Luke enjoyed the few pleasant hours with Chang and Jade, unaware that they would be the last serene hours he would know for some time.

Chang's brief appearance on TV news caused a great deal of amusement. Jade found it hilarious that her uncle acted so dignified when he wasn't that way at all. But there was little on the newscast they didn't know. Later, however, when they were enjoying Jade's "American-style dinner," fried chicken and mashed potatoes, this time over candles and flowers in the dining room, a half-hour special, hastily put together, of Jasper Dorn's rise to fame and fortune, contained a segment that was new. A film sequence of where the Dorn grandson was born.

The camera scanned the main street of a village in Montana, a short stretch of false-fronted stores, a cafe, a saloon and market, and came to rest on a small white modern building, the Silverleaf Clinic. A number of roughly dressed villagers were standing around curiously.

The off-camera commentator intoned, "This is where Christopher Dorn first saw the light of day, Silverleaf, Montana. We are waiting for the doctor who delivered the lucky child."

The camera focussed on the doorway and shortly a heavyset, stocky man with thick greying hair stepped out. His appearance and air of breeding and intelligence were such a contrast to the local people that the sound tract was silent in order to make the contrast more apparent. The doctor was wearing a somber suit and tie.

Then the commentator continued. "Dr. Stefan Vasa. . .may we have a few moments?"

Obviously the encounter had not been anticipated. The doctor squinted against the lights, stepped backward, then turned to face his unseen interviewer. "I was under the impression that no interview had been granted." There was controlled anger in his pallid face and heavily-lidded dark eyes. His voice was deep and markedly accented, Middle-European. "I am leaving."

"Just a few questions, Doctor." Ingratiating, patently insincere. "Have you heard of Jasper Dorn's death?"

"Yes."

"Have you any idea where Claire Dorn and her son are?"

"No."

The camera was focussing on the doctor's hands, hanging rigidly at his sides. They were beautiful hands, sensitive and strong, and webbed with fine scars.

"Could you tell us, Dr. Vasa, why are you living in this remote, backward village?"

Vasa's repressed anger emerged in scathing sarcasm. "Am I to reveal my soul's content to a thief? I value my peace and privacy." He pushed through the encircling group of local people and disappeared beyond the range of the camera's lens.

The camera lingered on the faces of the villagers who appeared resentful of the description of their village as backward. Then the film cut to a studio where a commentator, sitting at a desk, rapidly related the facts of Dr. Vasa's background.

He was of royal Hungarian descent. As a child of four, he had been forced into the Nazis' *Lebensborn*, *Leber*, light, *born*, source, Heinrich Himmler's program to attempt to breed an Aryan superrace. As time went on, the doctor did not conform to the perfect Nordic being, slender, blond and blue-eyed, and he had been sent to a youth home for appropriate "Germanization'' which was little more than a systematic destruction of rejected children.

"At the end of the war, Dr. Vasa's people found him. He recovered and went on to study medicine in Paris and eventually emigrated to the United States. Another example of Jasper Dorn's widespread interests is the generous endowment given to the Silverleaf Clinic when his grandson, Christopher, was born there.''

The film cut to some outside shots of the gleaming height of the Dorn Building in Los Angeles.

Chang switched the TV off.

Jade was shocked. "That man, he didn't want to be talked.''

"Talked to,'' Chang corrected. "What was the point of that?''

Luke was pouring wine. "With little else to film, I guess the networks had to find something.'' He was beginning to feel that the image Dorn projected was astutely continuing, after his death. He wondered who had given the network the information. Matthew Powell?

After dinner, Chang took Luke out to his garage greenhouse. He demonstrated it with some pride and a bewildering wealth of information. A free-standing structure with a Gothic arch. . .double strength glass panes for greatest light transmission. . .ventilation techniques. . .temperature controls with an alarm in Chang's bedroom to register temperature extremes or power failures. . .electric sensors. Chang confessed to doing his own watering.

Luke's head was swimming with the descriptions and the riotous color he saw everywhere. He marveled at a number of azalea trees that were as tall as his shoulder.

"They are my speciality,'' Chang said. "I water them with a solution of colchicine.''

"It sounds like a cough medicine."

Chang laughed. "It's an alkaloid, a poisonous substance derived from the autumn crocus and the meadow saffron. Centuries ago, royal gardeners used it in China. It doubles the normal number of chromosomes, resulting in cells with chromosome numbers that are multiples of the originals, resulting in hybrids which are also capable of reproduction and—"

Luke rubbed his forehead. "Forgive me, Chang. My head's throbbing now. I'll just say I think the azaleas are the most."

Chang grinned. "Colchicine is also used as a relief in gout, for some reason. No one knows exactly why." He plucked a withered blossom from one of the azalea trees. "I would grow them for their beauty alone but the additional income they bring provides me with the means, however small, to bring my family here."

"'A journey of a thousand *li* begins at one's feet,'"Luke quoted Chang's quote of Laotse. He liked the idea. It was a vastly comforting way to view life. Not as an uncharted infinity to be explored but a route to be chosen that seemed to be headed in the right direction. He said as much.

Chang was pleased. "I think our next immediate move is to go to bed." He stretched tired arms. "It's been a long twenty-four hours."

Luke agreed. And later, stretched out on the studio couch in Chang's study, he drowsily reflected on what a pleasant afternoon and evening it had been. He didn't know they were the last he was to have in some days.

A sharp rap in the door propelled Luke into a sitting position and he called out, "What's happened?"

The door flew open. Chang, already dressed in slacks and pulling a T-shirt over his shoulders, said with urgency, "Hurry, get some clothes on. Boyd has been shot and wounded. I'm deputizing you. We'll meet the other men up there. We have to search the grounds.''

As soon as the black and white shot across U.S. 1, the Hôtel's sirens could be heard. Apparently, whatever had happened, it had triggered the nursing home's security system. As they neared the gatehouse, the sounds of sirens were earsplitting. Scores of beamed lights illuminated the chalets and the peripheral grounds in a vast bubble of white fog like a towering incandescent iceberg. Shouting guards, some with Dobermans, others with walkie-talkies, were surging in and over the ragged halves of the wired steel gate. Boyd's sedate Datsun lay on its side, its smoking hood crumpled up against the shattered windshield. Boyd lay on a stretcher. Only his bleeding head was visible. Orderlies hurriedly thrust the stretcher into a waiting ambulance and its shrieking siren, as it streaked toward the Hôtel, swelled the earshattering pandemonium.

''Can't they turn those things off?'' Luke shouted to Chang who was slamming the driver's door. ''Wait here,'' he yelled. He dashed into the gate house where one of the guards was speaking repeatedly into a head-set microphone. He turned and barked out an explanation to Chang who immediately loped back across the road. He slammed the car into motion, gravel flying.

''Guards are already searching the grounds, procedures used in the event of a wandering patient. There's no point in adding to the confusion. I've sent my men home. So far they've found nothing. Boyd has a radio telephone in his car and he informed the gatehouse of his imminent arrival ten minutes before the guards saw his car make the last turn. When he was about a hundred yards away, he fell against the wheel, unconscious, and crashed into the gatehouse. No shots were heard but Boyd was hit in the right shoulder. A couple of inches higher and he would have had it.''

"This attack was premeditated. Someone wanted to kill him."

"It looks that way. We'd better get on up to the Hôtel."

When Chang parked by the main lodge, the sirens abruptly cut off.

"My head feels as if a truck ran over it," Luke said, swallowing and rubbing his ears.

Chang didn't comment. He was leaning forward intently, watching the entrance. The electronic doors were open and an orderly and a female nurse were attempting to restrain a tall, thin woman. Her hair was a tangled mess and she began to scream, her arms flailing the air violently.

"The patients," Chang said. "I'll bet it's bedlam inside."

No one noticed Luke and Chang when they entered, skirting the three struggling people. The woman was shrieking, "I won't! I won't go back in there. Take me home!"

Inside, several of the alcoves were occupied with orderlies and nurses and partially undressed patients. One of them sat dejectedly, head in hands, moaning, while another shrieked with mindless laughter. Another lay on the floor in an ashen faint.

Chang moved swiftly. "I'm going to the office. See if I can find Hilda Beck and learn how Boyd is. Why don't you look around? It's a good opportunity to explore the place."

As soon as Chang had disappeared, Luke walked toward the back to the carpeted corridors and the antiseptically gleaming halls. In the carpeted section some of the suites were vacant; others were occupied and most of the doors were open. He peered in one of them. A nude elderly woman sat in front of a wide mirror, smiling at her reflection. She was painting her flaccid skin with huge swirls of red lipstick. In a second suite, a young man in a voluminous white nightgown

57

knelt in prayer. When he saw Luke, he looked up with an angelic face and recited a glut of obscenities in the same reverent chant. Luke ducked away.

He had reached the end of the carpeted area and he passed into one of the antiseptically barren corridors. There were examining and treatment rooms in the first annex. But in the adjacent annex he knew he had found the cells Chang had described. This corridor was all but blacked out. The rows of doors were locked and each door was partially glassed. Inside the rooms were brightly lighted. He approached the nearest one cautiously and read on a slotted card, FEMALE, VIOLENT, 1470. He peered through the window.

The room was unfurnished except for a narrow bed that had a cage-like apparatus over it and a chest of handleless drawers. A young girl, although with the shaven head it would have been difficult to tell, and probably ten or twelve years old, sat handcuffed to a wooden arm chair. She was twisting and turning, straining against the wide band around her waist which confined her to the chair. She wore a knee-length wrinkled tan shift. Her arms and legs were covered with ugly reddening bruises. Saliva dripped from her mouth as she repeatedly bit her own tongue. It had begun to bleed and she licked at the blood, tasting it with slobbering pleasure. She repeatedly uttered strangled grunts and groans. She must have seen Luke for suddenly she spit toward the door and bloodied saliva splattered inside of the window.

A sourness filled Luke's mouth and, gulping for air, he hurried through the alcoved room which was almost deserted. He just made the car in time. He vomited near some bushes at the back of the car.

While he crouched there weakly in the fog, he heard an unfamiliar sound, rather like the plop of a suction dart when it hits the dart board. But instantly after the peculiar sound, the graveled soil at his feet flew wildly, showering his shoes and legs with pebbles. A second plop pinged sharply against the rear bumper. Luke didn't wait for a third. He dashed to the front of the car, jumped in and slammed the door.

The sounds had to be shots from a gun. A gun with a silencer. He rubbed his forehead with a trembling hand. It was wet with sweat.

At that moment Chang arrived. For once he seemed to have lost his air of detachment and his patience, as well. He slammed the door vigorously and crashed the car into motion. "The bullet in Boyd's back lodged against the clavicle. It's being removed now. But before he was put under, he issued orders that there was to be no undue publicity about the accident. He attributes the accident to another pointless act of violence. It's damned stupid. This attempt could well be connected with Dorn's death and I wouldn't be surprised if another attempt was made. He's senseless to risk his own life to protect the Hôtel's reputation."

They had reached the gatehouse and, while waiting for the improvised barricades to be removed, Chang looked at Luke. "What's wrong with you?"

Luke raised his head. "I think someone just took a couple of shots at me."

"You've got to be kidding."

"No." Luke described what had happened.

"Did you see anyone?"

"I didn't stop to look."

"It was probably one of the guards. He thought he saw something."

"The gun or rifle had a silencer on it. And no one heard the shots that caused Boyd's accident. It must have been the same guy. But why take a shot at me?"

"Maybe all the Hôtel firearms have silencers. That would be Boyd, not wanting to upset the patients. I'll check with Hilda about it."

Luke began to feel calmer. A guard had to be the

logical explanation. Or it might have been one of the patients. The disruption of the security system had given most of them a measure of freedom.

They were pulling up in front of Chang's home. He switched off the ignition and set the brake firmly. "You'd better pour yourself a stiff one. I'll call Hilda now."

Luke had taken a couple of hefty swallows by the time Chang had ended his call to Hilda. "She doesn't know anything about the security arrangements. But she'll ask Boyd when he comes to."

Luke gulped again. "Chang, that nursing home isn't a prison; it's a zoo. And that's being unkind to animals." He related what he had seen. "What happens to people? What turns them into parodies of human beings?"

Chang sat down. "I don't suppose there is a completely sane person in the entire world. Each of us functions irrationally to some degree. Or perhaps we function in spite of our irrationality. But the people who commit senseless acts, inspired by some illogical reason—"

"Insane, in other words."

"No, I don't think so. There are many kinds of reality. ESP has been a moonshot in the galaxy of the mind. Ancients and creative genius knew of it. Perhaps people are like radios, tuned into varying CB wave lengths. Most of us operate on the same wave length. But a few are tuned to some different band and, since they are psychologically unable to comprehend the symbols sent, they blow a tube or a compressor or something."

"And some of us come closer to blowing up than we realize," Luke said bitterly. "I don't suppose that's ever happened to you."

Chang traced the floral pattern on his teacup with a fingertip and said gently, "I can't say that it has. Why don't you tell me about it."

60

It was the only time Luke had spoken about Lori in detail to anyone. "My wife walked out on me. We'd been married about two years when we moved to the Coast and I began working at Dorn Enterprises. Something happened to us. We were both small-town Michigan, and Lori was exposed for the first time to men like Dorn, wealthy and powerful. She decided that I was a minor league operator. We had a no-fault divorce and she married a Greek who owns considerable real estate in his home town. I did my damnedest to keep her. Everything she wanted. Clothes, jewels, trips. I was in hock up to my ears."

Luke laughed deprecatingly. "Lori maintained I would never make it. So I decided I would really make it. Now, I'm still in debt and I haven't progressed an inch. Except maybe downhill. I missed out on a couple of promising situations. In fact, I think I could have moved up as Powell's assistant if I had worked the angles."

"So—"

"So I'm thirty-three and a washout. I was raised in an orphanage, Chang. I was lucky in one way. Scholarships, education. But I never seemed to possess anything, to belong. Lori was a symbol of everything I missed having. I loved her and the future looks as bright as a mudbath."

"So what is bugging you now?"

"It's obvious. If I had been smarter, Lori wouldn't have left me. I am just a minor league operator."

"Luke, go back to our CB analogy. Your wife sounds as if she were Foxy, Doxy Lady. But you are being Simple Simon."

"I get it, nothing between the ears."

"No. You are foolish because, through your love for her, you permitted her evaluation of you to distort your life. Ask yourself, what do you really want?"

It was a wrench to admit it, but Luke did. "To be a small town guy, out of the championship fight. Deal

61

with local environmental problems, not public images."

"Lori's leaving you was a gift of the gods. One should never frown on destiny. It isn't events, but our attitude toward events, that directs our lives. And that is destiny."

"But I can't swing it. My soul and salary are in hock for years to come."

"Once you decide what to do, the way will appear. There are fourteen of my nieces and nephews who have become American citizens. In Hong Kong they would have lived worthless, undeveloped lives. 'Tao is all-pervading. And its use is inexhaustible.' "

"Who is Tao?"

"I will attempt to explain another time."

"We always seem to be postponing conversations."

"But doesn't that imply we will have others?"

5

Was it destiny, Luke wondered, to have become involved in the most colossal Sunday traffic foul-up since the invention of the wheel? Chang would probably advise emotional calm—grin and bear it. To relieve the tedium of the past hour, cars inching in both directions near where the Hollywood and Santa Ana Freeways intersect, Luke grinned widely and toothily at the driver of a yellow Pontiac station wagon. They had been snailing along in tandem for some minutes. The driver, his face flushed and angry, snarled something and triumphantly shot ahead a few feet as his line of traffic began inexplicably to move more rapidly.

Luke won the war though. As they neared the cause of the tie-up, a massive truck and trailer which had jackknifed across the width of the freeway, he was able to angle in ahead of the station wagon where the four lanes dwindled to a single line, and he tooted his horn in victory. It was clear sailing from there to the Torrance exit and Palos Verdes.

Earlier that morning he had heard on KHJ radio news that Claire Dorn and her son had not been found. Anyone who might have information leading to their present address was asked to contact Matthew Powell at the Dorn Building in Los Angeles.

Luke switched off the radio, which at the moment was blaring rock music. Unfamiliar with Palos Verdes, he had to ask directions twice before he found the no exit street.

He parked the Mustang and eyed the house. It was built on three levels, high over rocky cliffs and thickly surrounded by dense shrubbery. There were balconies and turrets. A quasi hacienda of the type built in the early 1900's. It looked deserted, abandoned.

He was not hopeful of finding anything. Part way up the steeply curving drive, a for-sale sign had been nailed to a wooden post and underneath that in block letters someone had printed, WARNING, PREMISES DANGEROUS. When he reached the summit, he learned why. The rocky promontory upon which the house was built had partially fallen away. It was part of that widening section of California coastline which is slowly, but surely, slipping into the Pacific Ocean.

Hoping the house wouldn't choose that moment to take its fatal plunge, Luke circled the lower floor, a laundry and storage rooms, peering in dusty windows and trying doors. A narrow path led upward to the second level, a living room, and dining room with the kitchen at the back. He stood in a weed-infested patio and looked up. The third level with a wide balcony jutting out over the cliffs and sea must be the bedrooms.

In the patio, panes of glass in the French doors looked as if they had been systematically shattered. The doors were locked but he reached through one of the broken panes and managed to turn the self-locking door knob. When he stepped in, the musty, unclean odor was very strong. Colonies of spiders were flourishing. Cobwebs lined the arched doors to the dining room and the windows. The place had been completely looted. And what was left looked as if it had given refuge to a nomadic band of human pigs. Cans, empty bottles and crushed food cartons littered the living room floor and the blackened fireplace. Once it must have been lovely. A turquoise satin couch, now in tatters and probably too heavy to remove, graced one end of the long room. And the black and white kitchen, now spotted, cupboard doors broken, sink covered with piles of broken china, at one time must have been a young housewife's dream.

He climbed the narrow staircase to the two bedrooms which were in similar condition. In the smaller there were the remains of a crib and tattered bits of stuffed toys. Luke walked out to the wide balcony which joined the two bedrooms. Large ceramic urns were filled with dead foliage.

He stared at the view. It was magnificent. A smogless rarity. A row of fluffy clouds, like a procession of celestial ducks, dotted the azure sky. The dark outlines of Santa Catalina and San Clemente Islands intersected sky and a placid sea.

What kind of a young woman could Claire Dorn be? She must have walked away and left everything intact. Left it to destruction and decay.

He turned away from the view and stiffened. At the other end of the balcony there was a ragged gap in the wooden railing. He inspected it cautiously, peering down to the rocks and the foaming surf, far below. This must be the spot where Gilbert Dorn had plunged to his death.

Something creaked somewhere in the house and Luke hastily clattered down the narrow staircase. Outside he paused for a moment, evaluating what he had learned. Nothing. Nothing, except that this shocking abandonment was so at variance with what he had thought Claire Dorn was. A normal young woman, a loving wife and mother.

He heard another creak and walked rapidly down the curving drive. Eyeing the house furtively, he turned the ignition key. And swore. His car wouldn't start. He tried several more times with no success and then gaped in disbelief.

The hood of his car wasn't fastened. He knew he hadn't driven down from Belden Beach with a loose hood. Was it possible that someone had been tampering with the engine?

His impulse was to jump out and run but he forced himself to move out slowly. He proceeded to do what anyone would have done caught in similar circumstances. Walk to the nearest house for a telephone. He walked slowly, hoping with each step that a rifle wasn't aimed at his back and a bullet wasn't on its way.

It was a ghastly ten minutes and it seemed that he rang the doorbell of the modest stucco cottage endlessly before a round, young man, dressed in a blue Japanese robe, opened the door.

"God," he said. "Here's another one."

"Another what?" Luke asked shakily, moving as far inside as he could without seeming to.

"Police or detective. They've been haunting us all yesterday afternoon and this morning. So get lost. We don't know anything about J.D.'s death."

Luke introduced himself and briefly and breathlessly explained how he happened to be there. "I can't be sure someone was tampering with my car, but it sure as hell looks peculiar."

The young man looked Luke over with alert blue eyes. "Well, come in. You seem to be in, anyway. So you work for Dorn Enterprises?"

"I write the research section for the stockholders' quarterly report." Luke's legs felt weak and he coughed. His throat was so dry, it made speech difficult.

"Here. Take a swig of this." The young man poured a glass of orange-colored liquid from a pitcher. It turned out to be a mixture of carrot and apple juice, laced with soda to give it sparkle. "It'll set you up in no time. My name is Bob Fairway. I'm in insurance. During the day, of course. . .what were you doing up at the Dorn place?"

Luke gulped the last of his carrot-apple cocktail and felt better. "I'm looking for Claire Dorn. Do you know where she is?"

Bob Fairway frowned. "I think I'd better call Sara in on this. She sleeps during the day because she paints

66

at night. Better inspirational vibes.'' He raised his voice and called.

She appeared, yawning and peering through round, rimless glasses. She was wearing an identical blue Japanese robe. "How can I raise my levels when I can't get any sleep? What is it this time?"

Luke began an apology. "I'm sorry, Mrs. Fairway—"

"My name isn't Fairway," she snapped. "Not yet, anyway. It's Brown. We're both in the telephone book, listed separately. Everytime I remember it, I go cold. Wouldn't you think the telephone company could hyphenate Brown-Fairway? But, no. We had to arrange for two phones and two listings—"

"Sara, calm down. This is Luke Fremont. He works for Dorn Enterprises. He's looking for Claire."

Sara's round face tightened with suspicion and she and Bob exchanged a silent, significant glance. Pouring a glass of the vegetable cocktail, she said carefully, "We know—I mean, we knew the Dorns." She looked at Bob again.

Luke inspected the room. Circular water cushions took the place of furniture. There were large posters on the walls of contemporary rock stars and film personalities of the '30's and '40's whose magnetism have long since been replaced by low voltage TV robots. Luke detected the musty, sweet odor of marijuana. The rest of the wall space was covered with large canvases in great swirls of color. Sara's work, no doubt.

Both Sara and Bob were small people with short, mousey, home-trimmed hair and very young. They made Luke who was only a decade or so older feel ancient. But their significant glances and cautious attitude seemed to indicate that they might know something. They had all sunk to the water cushions which produced a rather melodic gurgle.

"So you knew Claire," he prompted tentatively.

67

"And Gil, before he died," Bob said.

"And that darling baby," Sara added. "I did a sketch of him when he was a month old. It's over there by the window."

Luke got up and examined it closely. The small sketch of Christopher was good. Really good. A cherub of a baby boy, propped against a pillow, a cluster of curls around his forehead, eyes half closed, and a subtly adult smile on his young mouth.

Presumably when his back was turned, his hosts had come to some decision about him. When Luke returned to his cushion, Bob cleared his throat portentously. Sara did also, less noisily. They were the personification of Lewis Carroll's Tweedledum and Tweedledee, alike as two peas in a pod.

"Yes, we knew them," Bob began. "And I guess it really starts with the trip we all took together. That was five years ago." He looked a bit astonished at the passage of time.

"It was a super trip," Sara said. "Just driving here and there." She turned to Bob. "You think we really should tell?"

"Yes, I do. It's a cold enchilada now."

And in bursts of contrapuntal narrative, they told Luke the story of the trip.

It seemed the four of them had no definite plans. They had decided to explore the West Coast, just let it all happen. And in this super fashion, they reached Silverleaf, Montana, a small mountain village. "Like no place you've ever seen." There was this creepy, crawly swamp. The four of them rented a dory, which they called their barge, because Gil liked to call Claire, Cleo. Their exploration was super until Claire-Cleo slipped in some gruesome mud and fell against the leaky barge. She started having labor pains the next night. Really heavy. Everyone thought, since she was only about five plus months P, that the birth would be premature. The birth was really really heavy.

"But the following day, the doctor. . .what was his name, Bob?"

"Vasa. Talk about a character in a Gothic movie—"

"Dr. Vasa told us that Christopher was full term. It happens sometimes, you know. P symptoms don't show up at first," Sara said with an air of ancient feminine wisdom.

"Gil was scared skinless." Bob mimed an expression of stark horror. "A full-term grandson would clue his dad in that they had been sleeping together before the wedding bells. Which was only six months before. Old puritanical Jasper would have gone right out of his gourd. J.D. was a hopeless case. Everyone sleeps together before the wedding. Right, Sara?"

"Of course. We've set the date for next January." She frowned. "Maybe."

"Darling," Bob protested, "no negative thinking."

She stared obstinately through her round glasses. "Sometimes the negative turns out to be the positive."

"Look," Bob said, "anyway you dig it, it's a cop-out of a tired question. Does anyone know why these two people should not be joined together in holy matrimony? If the Big Daddys in the white collars had asked the right question—Have you been to bed together?—there would have been no marriage. And a lot of religious and economic clout would have been lost. Think of it. No costly dispensations, no confessions, no guilts, no divorce laws or alimony or child support—"

"What are you talking about," Sara said heatedly. *"You're* the one who wants to get married."

Luke felt that the conversation had gotten out of hand. "I'll bet J.D. was wild when he heard about it."

Sara giggled. "You don't think Gil told his father the truth! He probably lied to J.D. from the time *he* was born. Gil told his father that the baby was premature and so Claire and Christopher stayed on in

Silverleaf for a month to give the supposed premie a chance to catch up.''

They fell silent for a moment. A shadow seemed to darken the sunlit room. Luke saw sorrow on their faces.

Bob sighed. ''A month later when Claire and the baby arrived, they looked wonderful. Then everything began to fall apart. The baby was sick all the time. Gil was boozing and Claire was antisocial. She fired their parttime maid and took care of the baby and that big house herself.''

''She wouldn't listen to anything we said. We were really like family. All she has is a brother who is an engineer in Australia.''

Bob stood. ''Luke, we think that J.D. learned the truth and racked Gil up for good. We suspect Gil deliberately jumped off that balcony. He just couldn't hack it.''

''Yes, but Claire is gutsy,'' Sara declared. ''She probably took the baby and split. To get away from that sickie, J.D. She didn't like him period. One day her car was there in the carport. The next day she was gone.'' Sara's lips quivered. ''She didn't even come to say goodbye. And then the for-sale sign was nailed up.''

''I just had a vibe!'' Bob shouted. ''Violent deaths. Gil and J.D. They're connected!''

''Oh, Bob, how wonderful.'' Sara looked radiant with approval.

''But where is Claire now?'' Luke prompted.

Bob frowned. ''We want to be sure that nothing's going to happen to her. We couldn't trust the police. Although I suppose they'll find her eventually. You've got to keep this to yourself, Luke.''

''I give you my word nothing will happen to her. After all, both Claire and her son will probably inherit a great deal of money. J.D. is dead.''

They nodded solemnly. Luke restrained a smile. No matter what your level of consciousness, money talks.

"Okay," Bob said decisively, "she's dancing in a disco in Hollywood with a rock group. It's really wild."

Luke was stunned. Claire Dorn, a mother and grieving widow, dancing in a disco? "You must be mistaken."

Sara shook her head. "No, we've seen her there several times. She looks different. Practically no clothes and lots of makeup. But there's her long hair. That great hair. Black black, like yours, Luke."

"She recognized us the first time but she didn't speak so we didn't either. Sometimes she just smiles a little as if she knows her secret is safe with us. Now, we've told you. And we'll cream you, Luke, if anything happens to her."

"It won't," Luke promised. He declined their offer to take him to the disco sometime that week. His weekend chores were finished. From now on the ball game belonged to Matthew Powell. "But you haven't told me the name of the disco." Luke saw their reluctance to reveal it.

"It's—it's called Venus," Bob said slowly.

Luke stood. It was time to be on his way and he was hungry, when he suddenly remembered his car. "Damn, do you think we can get a mechanic? On Sunday?"

Sara snorted and Bob offered to look the problem over himself. He knew something about cars; he had rebuilt their sports job.

Luke had an uneasy thought. "It might not be safe out there."

Sara snorted again. "Three's a crowd. Give us five minutes to change."

In less time than that they reappeared, wearing identical jeans and red T-shirts, and they all piled in the

71

red two-seater, Sara sitting on Luke's bony knees. When they reached the Mustang, Luke watched both ends of the deserted street. Sara stood, an unhappy expression on her round face, looking up at the Dorn house. And Bob, his head under the hood, muttered a litany of mechanical mysteries to investigate.

Suddenly he uttered a piercing whistle. "Man, are you lucky!" He held out a small object at arm's length.

"What is it?" Luke asked uneasily.

"It's some kind of plastic explosive. The only one I can think of is gelignite."

"Explosive!"

Bob bent to the engine. "Look. See those wires. They go to your ignition. You can jump on this kind of explosive and nothing happens. But give it an electrical charge and whoosh!"

Luke tried to say something and failed.

Sarah looked at the loose wires, turning an anxious face to them. "Then someone was trying to blow up Luke's car."

Bob nodded. "Yeah, with Luke in it. Only he returned to his car and must have practically caught the guy in the act."

Luke fought an impulse to sit down in the middle of the street. "Yesterday," he choked, "yesterday, I was shot at. We thought it was a mistake."

"Who's we?" Bob asked.

"Deputy Chang in Belden Beach where Jasper Dorn was killed."

"I'll be they're connected," Sara said rapidly. "But why?"

Luke shook his head. He was aware that both Sara and Bob were looking at him doubtfully and wondering now if they had been right in telling him about Claire Dorn. "Listen," he said, projecting an assurance he certainly did not feel. "I don't know what this is all about, but if anyone can figure it out, it's Chang."

"I think," Sara said, "we'd better get out of here."

Bob darted to the Mustang. "Just let me rewire the ignition."

After a hasty exchange of promises to keep each other informed in case a logical explanation was learned, Luke drove off to find a restaurant and a public telephone booth. Hoping the rare steak he ordered wouldn't arrive well-done, he called Chang.

"Someone tried to blow up my car. I practically caught him at it. It looks like I'm right in the line of fire. But why me? Shot at and now this!" He described what Bob had found.

Chang said nothing for a long moment. Then, "It does look as if the two incidents are connected. I talked with Hilda Beck this afternoon. Boyd told her the guards at the Hôtel carry conventional weapons. No silencers. That could indicate why Boyd was shot at and the security system was disrupted. A way to get at you in circumstances that would be called accidental. If so, someone must have known you were staying at my place and it would be logical to assume that you would be vulnerable during the emergency. Did you tell anyone you were staying here?"

"God, Chang, I'm not sure."

"I know I didn't mention it to anyone. If someone knew you were here, then you're being followed and you were traced to Palos Verdes today. Did you see anyone?"

"No," Luke groaned. "I'm fading out of the picture." Belatedly, he remembered to tell Chang about Sara Brown and Bob Fairway and the disastrous results, according to Bob and Sara, of Christopher Dorn's birth in Silverleaf, Montana. And Claire Dorn who, might, or might not, be dancing in a disco.

"Are you going to check it out?"

"No. I'll tell Powell tomorrow. He can deal with it."

"Keep me posted, Luke. And watch yourself."

"Will do." Luke hurried back to his table. The steak was done to the point of annihiliation, but he ate it. Even if it had been blood-rare, it would have tasted like rubber.

When he headed the Mustang toward Los Angeles, he caught himself eyeing the rearview mirror more than once.

6

At ten, Monday morning, the gleaming tower of the Dorn Building wasn't draped in black. But it might have been. From the gloved, uniformed doorman on up, employees walked softly and spoke in muted voices, like actors in a slow motion film sequence. Not that the machinery had ceased to function; the organization was too efficient for that.

Luke didn't stop at his office but went directly to Powell's, as requested. Luke was late. Upon arriving at his apartment the night before, he had found a huge azalea tree, dominating the center of the untidy room. He had examined it with pleasure. The shining leaves and billowing red blossoms were as large as his fist. A note, pinned to a branch, contained explicit instructions for its care and a message from Chang: "My cousin was pleased to deliver this token of friendship. I anticipate our next conversation." Luke had called Chang to thank him, but he was out and Jade promised to "repay" his message. In spite of his fluttering uncertainties about the attempts on his life, Luke had to smile.

But sleep had been elusive and, for once, it wasn't caused by futile regret about Lori. The events of the weekend had given rise to a latent desire to direct the course of his life. He suspected meeting Chang and appreciating the policeman's calm yet focussed attitude had something to do with it.

Staring at the dark ceiling, Luke decided that whatever the cause of the peculiar events, they emerged from the rarified strata of finance and power politics. Perhaps there was some dark secret about Dorn that Luke might have stumbled across. But it was a fact that this rarified world had destroyed his marriage and he wanted out.

It would be taking a most uncertain step on that journey of Chang's, but if Jade could travel thousands of miles to pursue a more rewarding life, which included learning a foreign language and adpating to an alien culture, why couldn't he risk a shotput of his own into the future?

The more he thought it over, the more imperative it became. Eventually he had reached a decision. In a month's time, perhaps less, after he had indoctrinated a successor, he would be free. Luke had slept well after that. Too well. He was a half hour late.

"Go on in," Powell's secretary said. "He's expecting you."

Matthew Powell was sitting behind his massive desk, which was piled high with papers. He looked as if he had spent the night there. His handsome, ebony face was drawn and tired. And he was disheveled, without his jacket or tie, and his shirt was wrinkled. He dismissed his assistant, who looked equally tired and suitably solemn.

"Luke, good to see you. I'm having a cup of tea sent in. How about you?"

"I'd prefer coffee."

Powell spoke into the intercom and, in a matter of seconds, his secretary had swooped in with steaming mugs.

"Would you hold all calls, Edwina, until we have finished?"

"Yes, Mr. Powell."

Matthew sipped, and some of the liquid splattered his desk. His hands were perceptibly trembling. Luke had never known him to be less than impeccably groomed or to lose his poised, superior manner which could be intimidating. Dorn's death must have been a devastating blow.

Powell rubbed his eyes. "Let's dispense with our reactions. We both know Jas' loss will be deeply felt by everyone who was associated with him. Perhaps

76

you'd better report on the weekend first.''

"You were right,'' Luke began. "There's more to Mr. Dorn's death than a mugging. I was shot at that same night Mr. Boyd was when his car crashed into the gate. And yesterday someone tried to explode my car.''

"I don't see the connection—''

"It's got to be connected with the Hôtel del Sol. That's why Mr. Dorn's body was moved up there and the reason for the attempt on Boyd's life.''

"But the police believe it was an accident. An act of violent hostility by one of the patients.''

"Matthew, Boyd referred to Mr. Dorn as Jas. They must have known each other. And it has something to do with the nursing home.''

Powell conjured up a patient frown. "It seems to me that's a naive clue. One of the inmates, a young man with a religious persecution complex, is being investigated. It seems he had made a number of threats on Boyd's life.''

It was Luke's turn to frown. Why was Powell so unwilling to accept his evaluation? That was partly why he had been asked to go to Belden Beach.

Powell sipped his tea. "There's no point in wasting time, speculating. The police seem quite competent and they are pursuing a creditable theory. It was what I had suspected. Due to Jas' aversion to physical impairment and the fact that his face was. . .mutilated, the motive for his death could be personal revenge. Someone, past or present, who hates him bitterly.''

"And a personal motive would rule out any political plot.'' What Powell was worried about was the Survival Kit legislation.

"Of course.'' Powell looked pleased that Luke had performed on cue. "Have you read Digby's libelous column in the *Times* this morning?''

"Not yet.''

"He states that Jas was killed because Enterprises

holds the reins on the enormous profits that the Kit will net. He claims he can name names of the vultures who want a share of the greatest hoax ever to be perpetrated on the American public. These adverse innuendos are hurting. Senator Farrow told me that members of both Houses have been deluged with letters and telegrams, protesting the passage of the bill. The hearings will certainly be influenced. Enterprises has millions tied up in pre-production costs and commitments. Obviously, the Kit isn't the ultimate answer to survival but it will have to do until something more comprehensive is developed.''

Luke wondered why he had ever been attracted by the machinations of power politics. Profit, but not loss. The blow dart of altruism could never penetrate its elephantine hide. Perhaps Powell's evident distress was due to his own secret knowledge of some manipulative scheme. Perhaps Powell himself stood to lose a bundle if the Kit bill didn't become law.

Powell coughed. ''Now, what did you find out about Claire Dorn?''

The abrupt change of pace took Luke by surprise. And the cough was a warning that Powell was leading up to something. ''I checked out the place where she lived in Palos Verdes. It looked as if she had walked out and left it there.''

Powell balanced a letter opener. ''So I was told. You see, to get back to the personal motive. We all know how Jas grieved over his son's death. And how proud he was of his grandson, Christopher. Yet a thorough search of Jas' personal files did not reveal an address on Claire. And not a scrap of correspondence with her was found. The police find it most peculiar that she hasn't come forward. It seems to indicate a rupture of their relationship. I also was told that Jas changed his will after Gilbert's death which is a further confirmation that Jas and Claire had some difference of opinion. The will goes to probate court next week but, until all of his heirs have been notified, names and content will not be released. It would be natural to assume that Christopher is one of the beneficiaries. You don't have any idea of where she might be?''

Luke hesitated. Although Powell hadn't actually said so, he had intimated that Claire might have a personal motive. If by any stretch of the imagination, she was the girl dancing in the disco, why hadn't she come forward? She couldn't help but know that Dorn had been murdered. Like Bob and Sara, Luke was beginning to wonder if she shouldn't be given a chance to state her reasons before being delivered to the media, the police and Powell. Luke knew that Powell wouldn't be put off by an evasive answer. But the unlikely truth would accomplish the same end.

''I heard that a girl answering her description is dancing in a disco, somewhere in Hollywood.''

Powell snorted incredulously. ''Another crank opinion. That was the trouble Sunday. People calling with a horde of false information. But you might tell Detective Franks about it. He's arriving shortly to question you.''

''What about?''

''It's obvious. I spent the greater part of Saturday at police headquarters being questioned. After all, except for his assailant, I was the last person to have seen him. You worked closely with him on research data. It's their business to check everything and everyone.''

Matthew finished off the last of the tea. His hands weren't shaking. He walked to the windows, standing with his back to the room in a dark and somehow brooding pose.

''What were you questioned about?'' Luke asked.

''My relationship with Jas. And a general picture of the shop. Personalities. Possible frictions.''

''What did you say about me?''

''Nothing derogatory. In fact, I emphasized that

since your wife left you, you've been out of things for the last few months. A loner, emotionally depressed. Belligerent.''

"How could my emotional state be important?''

"Now, Luke, you must admit you had several heated disagreements with Jas. Over final control of published research material.''

"But that was what I was hired to do. Mr. Dorn often made mistakes. He didn't understand a great many of the procedures.''

"But you did remark more than once to several people that it made you feel like an incompetent office boy.''

Score another hit for Lori, Luke thought angrily. He stood, propelled by some sense of imminent disaster.

Powell swung around, coughing several times. His evasive tension had been replaced by his usual superior manner, which always seemed the look of a man who has seen his enemy fall in a last burst of gunfire. "You should be grateful that I'm giving you a preview of the way authority thinks.''

Dazedly, Luke listened to further eccentricities of his behavior. Why hadn't he gone to Tony's Friday night, as he had for months? Luke remembered. Because he had gotten sloshed at home and later had played pinochle with his elderly neighbor. Sure, drinking would become another black mark against him. And Friday morning, the parking attendant in his apartment house had filled the gas tank in the Mustang. Why was the tank empty when the attendant had gone off at midnight? Probably, Luke thought, some little creep had siphoned it off. He had to force himself to clench his fists.

He said harshly, "I suppose the theory is I drove to Belden Beach, killed Dorn and shot back to L.A. If I had, my car would have been splattered with blood.''

80

"The hired car was used to transport the body to the nursing home. It was found in ghastly condition near the Costa Marina. And, if you recall, you weren't home when I first telephoned you."

Luke felt an explanation would be futile. Who would believe that anyone, so exhausted by lack of sleep and loss of self-esteem, would not hear the imperative ring of a telephone? In fact, he felt like the man in Kafka's *Castle*—every detail of his life controlled and manipulated by a malignant force that could be dimly perceived but never confronted. He now wondered if Powell had deliberately asked him to go to Belden Beach so the details of this unbelievable scheme could be worked out.

"Matthew, you can't believe this—this fantasy!"

"I'm sure no one believes it. You are simply someone who has to be checked out."

"Or have I been chosen to play the role of an alleged killer with a personal motive while the Survival Kit hearings are in session," Luke said savagely. "You must be insane."

Powell ran a hand over his close-cropped head. He gave the impression that he was restraining a yawn. "I suggest you use my office for your talk with Detective Franks. Yours has been sealed, pending further investigation."

"Why!"

"It is a matter of record that your wife left you in an embarrassing financial condition. A search of personal bank records revealed that Jas was being blackmailed. Substantial amounts over the past year."

Luke shouted, "You won't find any unexplained deposits in my depleted bank account!"

"Then how can you expalin that something over 10,000 dollars was found yesterday in your secret research data file?"

"What!"

"Luke, be reasonable. I fail to understand why you

81

are being so uncooperative.''

Luke headed for the door. My God, they were back at square one.

''Where are you going? I gave my word that you'd be here.''

''You know what you can do with your word,'' Luke shouted as he slammed the door.

Powell's secretary looked up nervously. ''Has your conference ended?''

Luke nodded. He couldn't have uttered a word.

''Good,'' she said. ''I've been holding a number of urgent calls for Mr. Powell.''

Luke forced himself to walk unhurriedly to the bank of elevators and into a waiting car. As he shot to the ground floor, reality dwindled to the expanse of Moorish tiled lobby which had to be crossed in order to reach the freedom of the smoggy, sunlit street. As he neared the lobby's entrance, the uniformed doorman was speaking into the house phone. ''Police Detective Franks to see Mr. Powell. He has an appointment.'' It was probably Franks who stood by the doorman, studying a racing form.

When Luke reached the sidewalk, his knees began to buckle. Dazedly, he realized he had to find a safe place where he would think. His apartment would be a trap. And so were the bars and restaurants where he was known. He couldn't go near his car. If Powell was so determined to make him a suspect, every patrol unit in the area would have his description and license number in a matter of minutes.

A half-empty city bus lumbered by. Luke sprinted and caught it at the corner before the red light changed to green. The driver, obviously annoyed that he had to reopen the doors, sneered pleasantly when Luke couldn't find the exact change and had to overpay the fare. At the back, he found a seat and huddled in a corner, breathing hoarsely.

7

An all-points bulletin was issued by the LAPD just before noon on Monday morning that Luke Fremont was wanted for questioning. Chang, who had celebrated his first day of vacation with an early morning, leisurely swim, learned of the APB when he called the substation to ask if his homeowner's insurance policy had been mailed there by mistake. Surprised and worried, Chang went out to his greenhouse. He had decided to build a small shed at the back to accommodate tools and other equipment. Since methodical labor is conducive to reflective thinking, Chang had intended contemplating his own problems, mainly his imminent retirement, but his concern about Luke dominated his thoughts.

Chang's initial reaction had been one of incredulity. And careful recollection only confirmed it. He was convinced that Luke was not involved in Dorn's death. Chang could not believe that there were any serious charges against the younger man, so it meant that something had occurred, probably during the meeting with Matthew Powell, that had spurred Luke to rash and hasty flight. However, Luke most certainly would be arrested, and Chang wondered what could be done to avoid it.

A telephone call to Sheriff Mintner would probably accomplish little. It might be construed as unprofessional interference. Eventually Chang decided that a call to Matthew Powell would do no harm and it might help. To his surprise, instead of expressing a loyal interest, Powell sounded coldly indifferent.

"I fail to understand why you are telling me. The matter is quite out of my hands. Fremont's refusal to be questioned is strange. A man with nothing to hide would have availed himself of the opportunity to clarify his position.''

''Surely, Luke isn't suspected of having killed Mr. Dorn?''

''No. At least, I don't think so. But he did mention he might know where Claire Dorn is. The fact that she has so mysteriously vanished is again strange. There is a possibility of collusion.''

Powell wouldn't say any more.

Chang returned to the pile of lumber but found himself sitting on a nail keg, doing nothing. Powell's inferences began to take on a sinister aspect. Luke had learned only yesterday from Sara Brown and Bob Fairway that she might be dancing at the disco, but Powell was hinting at collusion.

Mid-morning, Chang's telephone rang. It was Sheriff Mintner. ''What's this I hear about you telephoning Matthew Powell?'' he rasped.

''Luke Fremont isn't involved in Dorn's murder. He was pursuing a line of inquiry for Matthew Powell. Luke was shot at and Sunday someone put an explosive in his car.''

''Oh, yeah.''

''Listen, Sheriff. So far, everything seems to focus on the Hôtel del Sol. It could be very important.''

''Chang, it's none of your business to decide what is important and what isn't. Fremont is wanted, officially, to fill in some of the details. Like why was 10,000 dollars found in his office files? You're not connected with the investigation and never will be. So keep your nose out of it.''

''I understand.''

''Do you have any idea where Fremont might be?''

''No.''

''Well, if you hear anything, report it to me, at once.''

Chang replaced the receiver thoughtfully. The

10,000 dollars in Luke's files had to be some kind of a macabre joke. Who had put it there? Powell? Maybe. Powell certainly hadn't lost any time in informing Mintner that Chang had called him. Why? It looked as if Powell was determined to see Luke discredited and without support.

All Chang could do was hope that Luke had enough trust and faith in their brief friendship to get in touch with him.

Late afternoon, Chang was tending a smashed thumb under the faucet at the watering trough when the telephone rang again.

He grabbed it, hoping it was Luke, but it was Hilda Beck, calling from the Hôtel. She spoke softly as if she did not want to be overheard.

"Chang, do you know where Luke Fremont is?"

"No."

"I think it's dreadful. The news about his being wanted. I heard it on the radio. He couldn't be connected with these dreadful events."

"I couldn't agree with you more."

"Avery hasn't heard about it. He wants to talk to Luke. Someone was in the Hôtel Sunday night. I think it was another attempt on his life."

Hurriedly, Hilda explained. Someone had broken into the kitchen wing which was not covered by the security system in the Hôtel proper. Unable to move from that wing, the intruder had started a fire. Fortunately, it had been discovered immediately.

"But I managed to convince Avery that it was the same person who shot at him. He's deeply troubled, Chang. And he has agreed to tell Luke what he knows."

Without a second's hesitation, Chang suggested that Boyd talk to him. "Hilda, I'm not connected with the investigation. Assure your brother of that, unless I have his permission, I will not reveal what he tells me.''

''I'll try,'' she said doubtfully.

Chang cradled the receiver. With Boyd being so secretive, there was little chance that Mintner would hear of it. But it certainly indicated that there was a connection between the Hôtel and Dorn. He heard Hilda's breathless voice.

''Avery has agreed. Not tonight though. He's too ill and tired. Tomorrow morning at ten. But not at the substation. And no one must be with us.''

''I'm on vacation so come to my home. Jade will be shopping in the city all day. Park behind the greenhouse. Your car can't be seen there from the street.''

Chang worked like a fury after that on his shed. It was even possible that Boyd's information might lead to a solution of Dorn's murder. The cloud over Luke would disappear and such an achievement would certainly solve the problems of his own bleak future. Chang sat up late that night, waiting for a call from Luke. He wanted to share the promising development. But Luke didn't call.

Hilda Beck and L. Avery Boyd were late by a half hour. Hilda parked behind the greenhouse, as instructed. Chang hurried out, offering assistance and leading the way over the uneven path to the back door of his house. In the living room, Boyd fell into a chair, passively accepting his sister's maternal attention, smoothing his thinning hair, adjusting the sling on his right arm. His obsequious self-assurance had deserted him. He wore sun glasses and was so swathed in car robes he was almost unrecognizable. His face was emaciated and pale. A bandage covered one eye; the other, swollen and bloodshot, darted about nervously. He was the picture of a badly frightened man.

''Thank you, Chang, for seeing us,'' Hilda began. ''I'm sure when Avery reveals what is troubling him, he will feel much better."

Her statement was obviously designed to encourage Boyd to talk who was just as obviously reluctant to begin. He stared at Chang for some time. Chang was wearing his gardening clothes and the absence of an official uniform seemed to help Boyd. In a reedy, quavering voice, he rambled on about his efforts, over the years to establish the Hôtel's reputation for privacy and exclusivity.

Chang prodded gently. "But you did know Jasper Dorn."

"Yes." Boyd's fingers plucked nervously at the fringes of the car blanket. "But I want assurance you will not report this to the authorities. I am guilty of nothing. Nothing!" he said fiercely. "If anything, I am a victim, too."

"You have my word."

Boyd's surge of strength appeared to have left him. He slumped back and began to speak in a rapid, low voice as if his story had been mentally rehearsed.

"Twenty years ago I managed a nursing home in Texas. Jasper Dorn brought his wife there. She was subject to severe depression which was the result of an extramarital affair. The man with whom she had been involved, Dorn's partner at the time, had committed suicide and her own unstable nature, schizoid tendencies, had collapsed under the weight of the righteous intolerance Jas was well-known for even in those days. I pointed out that with intensive psychotherapy she might recover. After all, she was a mother and their son Gilbert was only seven. But Jas wouldn't hear of it. Politically ambitious and excessively concerned about his public image, he wanted her out of his life completely. Her death must have been a relief to him."

Chang wondered if Boyd, through shock and fear, was magnifying a former and irrelevant connection with Dorn into some immediate threat to his life.

Boyd continued more slowly. "History repeats itself. Shortly after his son's accidental death, Jas telephoned. I hadn't seen him in years. It was a cryptic conversation. He wanted—he ordered me to send an ambulance to his home in San Fernando Valley. The ambulance was to pick up an individual whom he was entering as a patient in the Hôtel."

Boyd faltered. He asked his sister for a glass of water. It seemed an interminable length of time before he got his voice under control. "Since Jas had requested that he be admitted to the grounds without identifying himself, I was waiting in the gatehouse and I rode up to the lodge in his car. Naturally, I demanded to know the identity of the patient."

Boyd covered his eyes. "Jas told me it was his grandson, Christopher."

Chang was stunned. A baby, an inmate in that prison!

"I refused to admit the child. He was only six months old. Dorn said nothing. Simply sat there, waiting in the car, while the stretcher with the child was carried into the Hôtel to one of the private suites. The child was still unconscious when Jas and I entered the bedroom. He had insisted on sedation during the trip. I removed the sheet covering the boy."

Boyd faltered again but looked up. His eyes seemed filled with a kind of terror. "I'm not a doctor. Certainly not an obstetrician. But the child could have been well over a year old. Perhaps more. Yet his chronological age was barely six months. His body was proportionately formed. But his head and extremities were grotesquely enlarged. More than twice the normal size. A handsome face, except for its horrifying size."

"What was wrong with him?"

"Jas had brought two previous medical diagnoses. The child had a pituitary imbalance. He was already showing the evidence of acromegaly. A rare disease. Gigantism. Characterized by rapid growth, enlarged

88

head and extremities and thickened skin, particularly on his feet. He had a voracious appetite. As time went on, he grew so rapidly, he almost seemed to change daily and he became virtually uncontrollable. He was incredibly strong and subject to violent rages. A male nurse was with him 24 hours a day and he had to be kept under constant restraint.''

In one of the illuminated cells in the back annex, Chang realized with shock, that Luke had seen.

''Christopher couldn't speak beyond a hoarse mewling, possibly due to atrophy of the vocal chords or a failure of the larynx to develop properly. It was never determined. For more than a year, there were innumerable expensive tests, bioassays, x-rays, glandular treatments, specialists in every field of medicine. I never knew who they were. Jas arranged the consultations. But no hormonal imbalance was revealed. Not a single test or treatment was effective.''

Hilda uttered a shocked gasp and took a handkerchief from her purse.

''Twice his feet were operated on to remove the thickened skin. It grew back both times. Psychoanalysis was impossible due to his inability to communicate. The doctors were never certain how much he could comprehend, although he could understand simple sentences when he chose to.''

Hilda gasped again. ''Avery, I can't believe it.''

''Please, Hilda,'' Boyd said impatiently. ''He was a powerful swimmer. Water seemed to fascinate him. Calm him. His only other interests were watching television and leafing through picture books his mother sent him. For some reason, he always destroyed the toys she sent. Except for the boats. He would float them in the swimming pool.''

''His mother must have been frantic,'' Chang said.

''I don't know what she felt. Claire Dorn never came to see him.''

''That's impossible!''

"But it's true. Except for the gifts, she apparently had no interest in her son's condition."

Hilda was crying softly.

Boyd attempted a pathetic smile. "Don't you see? Jas was determined to conceal the fact that his grandson had a rare and incurable disease. All that could be done for the boy was to feed and wash him and hope mercifully that the inevitable physical and psychological deterioration would end his miserable existence. And, oh God, he grew and grew."

Chang tried to convince himself that this bizarre tale couldn't be true.

"One afternoon, about a year ago, the boy was swimming, naked in the pool. Alone, of course. I never allowed other patients to swim with him. He was then chronologically four and a half years old but he appeared to be about ten. When the male nurse left an orderly in charge for a few moments, Christopher beat the orderly unconscious with one of his sail boats, held him under water until he fainted. Then dressed in the orderly's clothes—not the shoes, his feet were too large—he disappeared in the grounds. By the time his escape was discovered, he had climbed the wall and vanished. Subsequently, the orderly died."

Chang experienced a flash of insight. "The orderly's name was Groder. Felix Groder."

Boyd looked puzzled for a moment. "Of course, you investigated what seemed to be a mugging on the beach. That was where Jas told me to move the body."

Chang was dismayed. Boyd was not innocent. He had obstructed justice in concealing the truth about Groder's death. And Captain Leo Stone had been right. Groder had died up at the Hôtel.

Boyd's voice rose hysterically. "Don't you understand? It would have been the headline of the century. A four-year-old child who looked like a monster, throttling an adult male and escaping. The Hôtel's reputation would have been destroyed. Jas was more determined than I that the existence of the boy be kept from the media and the police. Don't you see? Someone knows the boy was a patient in the Hôtel. That person killed Jas and is out to ruin me. Or kill me, too. And the only person I can think of who knew and would hate both of us is Claire Dorn.''

Chang stared. ''You said she was indifferent to her son's welfare. She never visited him.''

''She might have been forced to stay away. Jas had committed the boy and was responsible for payment. He could have withheld visitation rights. I now suspect that he did.''

Chang pointed out that Claire Dorn was physically incapable of killing and transporting Dorn.

Boyd screamed. ''Of course, she is incapable. But she could have confided in some man who is physically capable. And she's had a year to figure out a way to avenge five years of suffering. I never met her but once she sent a picture of herself to her son. She looked like a lovely, sensitive and determined young woman. The child tore up the picture, of course.''

''Do you think the boy is alive?''

''No. That was one point the doctors agreed on. The extraordinary growth inhibits proper development of vital organs and susceptibility to disease becomes inevitable. Besides, he was malformed, unable to speak. There might have been a few dollars in Groder's pockets but he might not have known what it was. Beyond what he might have learned from television, he knew nothing of the world. And where could he have gone, unnoticed?''

''So I imagine after a certain time, you and Mr. Dorn assumed he was dead and Claire Dorn was informed.''

''Yes. And with her son dead, she was no longer under any prohibition Jas might have imposed on her. She could have revealed everything. But she didn't. And why? Because she planned to kill both of us.

Revenge." Boyd fell back, closing his eyes. He looked exhausted.

Hilda whispered, "God forgive you, Avery."

Boyd ignored her. There were tears on his sallow cheeks. "You've got to help me, Chang. I refuse to permit any of this information to be released to the authorities. If you do, I shall deny everything. But you must find Claire Dorn and she must be given a full explanation. I provided professional services. It was Jas who laid down all the ground rules. I must save myself and the Hôtel."

"If she is behind this, as you suspect, she would have to be convinced that her son did receive the best treatment. Do you have any records to prove it?"

Boyd shook his head wearily. "All records were destroyed after it was safe to assume the boy had died. I did send a box of picture books to her which she never acknowledged."

"But if she is confronted with what you have told me, and is the person behind all this, she can deny her son was ever a patient in the Hôtel. And that leaves her free to ruin or destroy you."

Boyd groaned.

"Perhaps someone else knew that the child was Dorn's grandson," Chang suggested, aware that blackmail, not death, would more likely be involved.

"No. The child was isolated completely and I told you patients are identified by number only. Their names are coded on microfilm and in my office which is triple locked."

Chang was reminded again of the time when Boyd's office was flooded with water. Anyone on the staff could have gotten in. But he said nothing.

Boyd closed his eyes again. "All the specialists who were called in weren't told the child's name or, if they were, Jas arranged for their silence. And only the male nurse knew that the child killed Groder."

"And where is the male nurse?"

92

"Jas saw that he was financed and he left the country. I have no idea where he went. I tell you, Claire Dorn is behind this!" Boyd began to cough and gasp uncontrollably.

Hilda Beck wiped her eyes, blew her nose and efficiently, if in a resigned manner, helped her brother to stand. "Avery, you've talked enough. You need a rest. Thank you, Chang."

Chang stood. "I would advise that this be told to the authorities immediately."

"No," Boyd muttered. "Never!"

Hilda said impatiently, "I don't think you are capable right now of deciding what should be done. I pray it will sort itself out in time. Chang, do you know where the young woman is?"

"Possibly. I'm not sure."

"If you can, will you talk with her?"

"I'll have to think about it."

Hilda nodded. "It can be to Luke's advantage, too, if the truth is discovered."

"I know."

A moment later Hilda's car started up and drove away.

Chang wandered out to his greenhouse, hoping to find solace in the purity and beauty of his plant world. He felt sickened and appalled. Boyd's bizarre tale had to be true; he was fighting for his life and his livelihood. But what did it all add up to?

Because of Jasper Dorn's overwhelming conceit, ambition and desire for power, his grandson was dead, Boyd was threatened with ruin, if not death. Claire Dorn, once a normal young wife and mother, appeared to have become a bitter, revengeful woman. Luke Fremont was a fugitive from false arrest, charges which could ruin his life. And, if proof could be found, L. Avery Boyd would be indicted as an accessory in Groder's death; Claire Dorn might be charged with murder.

93

And Chang, himself? No matter whether he withheld the information or revealed it, he was guilty of unprofessional conduct and breaking the laws he had sworn to uphold. He should have never listened in the first place or promised silence.

During the early afternoon, he reviewed the salient facts in Dorn's death and Boyd's information and irrelevant flaws began to emerge. Who had shot at Luke up at the Hôtel and who had attempted to blow up his car? If Claire Dorn had plotted with an accomplice to kill her father-in-law and Boyd, why add Luke to the list?

The urgency to talk with Luke was agonizing. Why couldn't he summon up enough trust in Chang to risk a telephone call?

It was a long and unpleasant afternoon. Chang forced himself to begin preparing the monthly delivery of plants for his cousin's shop in Los Angeles. The hybrid azaleas were unusually fine. As he stood back to admire a bushy pink tree, he had an errant thought.

If Christopher Dorn had survived, he would be about five, almost six years old. In view of his previous extraordinary growth in size and deformation of extremities, how monstrously large would he have become and how violent? Chang shuddered.

He worked until Jade called out that dinner was almost ready. When he was seated at the table, she began an animated account of her day's shopping in Los Angeles, describing her new clothes. Chang found he couldn't concentrate. During the long afternoon, he had debated whether or not to take Boyd's information to Sheriff Mintner. And now he decided that he must do so. His promise to Boyd would be broken, but his integrity as an officer of the law preempted his word as a man. He decided that, as soon as they had finished dinner, he would make the call.

When the telephone rang, Jade answered it. Chang hoped that the caller was Luke.

Jade frowned. "It's for you, Uncle. Sheriff—?"

Mintner! Chang took the receiver, attempting to compose his thoughts. But he couldn't speak a word. Mintner was raging.

"Hilda Beck just called me from the Hôtel del Sol. She's coming in tomorrow to make a full statement. Her brother, Boyd, told her that the Dorn grandson was a patient in the nursing home. She says it was told to you this morning. How come you didn't report it to me?"

"I was told in an unofficial capacity."

"Unofficial, hell. It was your duty to pass on the information."

"I advised Boyd to report it."

"You're guilty of dereliction of duty, Chang. And what's more, a plant sent by you was found in Fremont's apartment. What the hell is going on?"

"He had admired them. I sent him one."

Mintner snarled. "Did it ever occur to you that this investigation isn't about some kook out there at the commune? Dorn was a very, very important man. Every detail, no matter how small, will be blown up all out of proportion. The federal guys are on my neck. Jesus, you make a police officer look like a goddam queer. If the press hears about your behavior, concealing relevant information, defending a wanted man and sending him potted plants with a queer message. . .looking forward to our next conversation—"

"It was an act of friendship."

"Yeah, but what kind of friendship? Matthew Powell is trying to get a line for us on why Fremont's wife left him. Maybe this is the answer. And maybe Dorn found out about it. He wasn't a man who would tolerate a goddam queer working for him."

"And I've reached the end of my tolerance, Mintner," Chang said slowly.

"Listen, Chink. There'll be no departmental announcement of it. Gotta keep it out of the papers. But you're on suspension. And when your vacation is over, there'll be an inquiry into your conduct. I wouldn't be surprised if the advisability of retiring you on full pension is re-evaluated.''

When Chang hung up, he was breathing hard. He left the dining room hurriedly, ignoring Jade's anxious glance, and went to the patio. Plants could react to human emotion and his thoughts were so black and beastly, he wouldn't have been surprised if every plant in the house had begun to wither away.

Bit by bit, his anger diminished and he was able to think rationally. It appeared that Matthew Powell was subtly but relentlessly stage-managing events, which would discredit or destroy Luke. The unexplained money in his office files which had goaded him to flee. And now this innuendo of sexual deviation. Did the shots at the Hôtel and the explosive in Luke's car indicate that Powell intended to provide the police with a dead suspect? Was it possible that Powell killed Dorn or knew who had?

"Uncle, I've warmed your dinner again," Jade said. She looked at him worriedly as he sat down. She was presiding at the *wok* and the fragrance of delicately broiled shrimp and shredded vegetables was tantalizing. Chang took an appreciative bite. But his face was gloomy and forbidding.

"What's wrong? Isn't the food prepared to your liking?"

"No, child. It's perfect. I have just re-evaluated my attitude of agreement with Laotse in regard to *wu wei*. There are times when interference is vitally necessary."

Chang had decided to do everything possible to learn who had killed Dorn and why. There was a powerful weapon left to him. With no departmental announcement of his suspension, Barker at the substation would continue to be a reliable source of official information.

8

His park bench was not very comfortable and probably not very safe. But the park was small and fairly dark. Half of the scattered corroded lamp posts were unlit. And after having spent most of the day on the Greater Los Angeles crowded transit system, the motionless bench might have been made of feathered down. The incessant chirp of crickets was comforting, reviving boyhood memory, campfires and a lake. But Luke could not concentrate on the antiphonal melody for long; bewilderment and anger returned to engulf him.

That morning, after a quarter of an hour on the first bus—and that seemed a century ago—it had occurred to him to wonder where it was going. The driver informed him they were headed south and in about forty-five minutes would return north on the same route. At the end of the southern leg, Luke had transferred to a line going east. And, except for a nervous lay-over for a late lunch in a small cafe in Inglewood, he had managed, by asking directions or relying on lucky guesses, to reach the northern fringes of Hollywood and the haven of the small park.

His decision to go to the disco Venus where Claire Dorn might be dancing was the result of an incoherent carousel of thought which had careened between livid rage at Matthew Powell and incredulity that he was embroiled in such an unbelievable situation.

At first, his single overriding purpose was to avoid arrest which would transform him into a murder suspect, fingerprinted, photographed and shown on the seven o'clock news. Luke did not intend to be subjected to humiliations that were probably worse than he could imagine. If Powell hadn't slipped up and given him a preview of what the police had in mind, he might at that very moment, be staring at the walls of a cell.

And then it hit him. Powell was too astute to have alerted him without reason. Powell must have wanted him to panic!

The empty gas tank and his non-appearance at Tony's could have been explained. But how to account for the 10,000 dollars hidden in his files? Powell must have put the money there to nail him with a personal motive for blackmail and murder. But Powell didn't want him arrested. He wanted him on the run so that a fatal shot on a foggy night or an exploding car would establish his guilt without trial and effectively conceal whatever it was that threatened the Survival Kit legislation.

Eventually Luke was able to channel his mind into the nuts and bolts of his incredible predicament. He could think about practical matters. Money? He had about fifty dollars in his wallet. Not enough, by far. A cash advance on credit cards? Too risky. His name and the location where the transaction had taken place would exist for someone to find. He longed to contact Chang who was the only person he could think of who would take this nightmare seriously. But Chang represented the law and had to be avoided.

It was then that he had remembered Claire Dorn. He had seriously doubted that she was the girl dancing at the disco; now he desperately hoped she was. There had to be some reason for her refusal to contact the police. Perhaps she could come up with some answers.

He had walked by Venus earlier in the evening. At one time the disco must have been a small local motion picture theatre. There were no photographs in the glass case by the entrance. Just an announcement, SQUARES COME AT SEVEN: SWINGERS, AT ELEVEN. So Luke assumed that the real show didn't begin until the later hour. He still had the better part of an hour to wait and decided to have something to eat. He could foresee that food and sleep, even a shower, were now essentials to be sought.

The drop-outs, runaways and rebels did not take any particular notice of him in the instant food bar. But he had the irrational fear that everyone was looking at him and knew who he was. And he desperately wished for information, but the coin-operated newspaper box outside was empty. By the time he arrived at Venus, a line of impatient young people was waiting to be admitted. Luke joined the line.

When he reached the door, he learned from a host, who was effeminately dressed in white boots, a fringed blue jacket and suede pants, that admission was by membership card only. There was nothing effeminate about the host's size. He topped Luke by a good two inches, and he listened aggressively to Luke's hesitant explanation that Bob Fairway had suggested he look the place over. Luke was admitted, not to the disco rooms, but to a small office, cleverly concealed by a jungle of synthetic trees, hung with twinkly Italian lights. But even the office seemed to vibrate with disco sound, the heavy back beat and up tempo of the Silver Convention. The music was taped sound and, if there wasn't a live rock group appearing, there would be no alleged Claire Dorn dancing there. Luke feared to inquire of the young woman in a grey turtle neck sweater over red shorts, who studied him impersonally through heavy hornrimmed glasses. Her face was pale and unadorned. She looked as out of place in a disco as a football player would have on a tennis court.

"My name is Percy," Luke improvised hastily, his boyhood memory still in the background of his thoughts. He hoped he didn't look as grimy as he felt. "I just moved here from Chicago. Bob Fairway steered me here."

She explained indifferently that personal and business references were required in the event he wished to apply for a membership. She gave him a courtesy card which entitled him to drinks on the house.

He wandered into the nearest bar and ordered a vodka collins. From what he could see and gather from the bartender, who shouted over the throbbing din, Venus had everything. Recreational areas, pinball, backgammon and pool rooms, a superior restaurant. But the dance floor and dancers were the heart of the disco. From where Luke sat, the large room could be indistinctly seen through clouds of synthetic swirling fog, illuminated by strobe lights in a revolving spectrum of color. Laser beams of red and yellow gave life and movement to the gold prisms on the ceiling. The women were elaborately dressed in long skirts with bare backs and shoulders, and most of the men were nude from the waist up. They danced languidly in erratic patterns.

The taped music cut off abruptly and a voice rasped over the PA system, announcing the imminent appearance of the Zodiacs. A rock group materialized on a narrow stage. The four men wore sequined loin cloths, tribal headdresses and gold platformed sandals. Their faces and bodies were painted with symbols of the zodiac. The beat of their music was primitive, drums and harsh, discordant electric guitar. The song had no lyrics, only the sensual rise and fall of repetitive indistinguishable cries, interspersed with a single shouted phrase, "Venus make me die! Venus make me die!"

The music cut off momentarily, and the lights dimmed. And under a single spotlight, a figure grew luminously brighter. Patrons were chanting, "Venus! Venus!"

Luke stared. Except for strategic circles of glittering gold, the girl was nude. A thin, sexless, swaying body. Glossy black hair fell about her bare shoulders. Her head was thrown back, eyes hidden beneath heavy smoky eyelids and enormously elongated black lashes. The music took up the beat again and, in quickening tempo to the discordant cries, she danced. It was so uniquely a simulation of sexual fervor that Luke found his senses responding.

"Who's the gal?" He asked the bartender who shrugged. Luke turned back to watch her. The girl simply could not be Claire Dorn. No cosmetics or choreography could have created such a transformation.

In a final apocalyptic movement, the dance reached a climax. No one applauded; it was not the "in" thing to do. But an appreciative murmur filled the room.

The girl stood quietly, humbly, arms slightly raised and stripped of her dancer's tension. She smiled and the sex goddess was given mortal identity. It was Claire Dorn.

The illuminated stage darkened and dissolved into striated light and fog once more. Its disappearance created the illusion that she might vanish, too. Standing quickly, Luke saw her entering a lounge room. He stumbled across the dance floor as quickly as he could and found her. She was huddled in one of the low cushioned chairs, head resting against the back of the seat. Her eyes were closed. She had pulled on a sheer robe, and her face and the robe were damp with perspiration.

"Great dance," Luke said. "Can I bring you a drink?"

"No," she said indistinctly. "Thanks." Her eyes were still closed.

"I know friends of yours. Sara Brown and Bob Fairway."

She opened her eyes angrily. "Will you leave me alone. Go away."

Rimmed by the mask of eye shadow and mascara,

the pupils were dilated. She must have been taking drugs of some kind. She was another Lori of the world, Luke thought in sudden rage and disgust, intent on doing her own thing and to hell with her responsibilities to her son. He held her shoulders roughly and shook her.

"You're Claire Dorn. Damn it. Admit it!"

He was unprepared for her recoil and wide-eyed stare of fear. In seconds she had whirled to her feet and had almost reached the door. Luke caught her by an elbow. She struggled.

"Your father-in-law is dead. Murdered."

"Let me go!"

"Why haven't you gotten in touch with the police?"

She tried to bite his hand. "I'll scream and you'll end up in jail."

"If you don't help me, I might end up in jail anyway."

She stopped struggling. "What does that mean?"

"It seems I've been hand-picked as a stand-in for Dorn's killer."

"Who are you?" She frowned and tried to focus her eyes. "You're Luke, Luke Fremont." She attempted to twist away again, more vigorously.

"Look, I'm in a hell of a mess. I'm trusting you so why can't you trust me? You've nothing to fear from Dorn. He's dead."

"I know Jasper is dead. And I'm glad. Glad!" She swayed and almost slipped out of his arms.

A sparsely clad couple had entered the lounge and was watching them curiously. Then the blue suede-suited host stood at the door. "Everything, okay, Venus?"

"Yes, Roy."

The host disappeared, and Luke whispered urgently, "Where's your car? We can talk there."

She gave him a long unfocussed stare, then moved

102

docily toward the back, down an unadorned corridor. In one of the dressing rooms, she dazedly collected a pouch purse. "Keys," she said thickly. She guided him, but he had to support her through the darkened parking lot to a tired-looking Fiat. Luke deposited her in the car and climbed in behind the driver's seat.

"You are Claire Dorn, aren't you?"

She nodded.

"Why haven't you gotten in touch with the authorities?"

When she spoke, he could scarcely hear her. "Because I swore I would never have anything to do with Jasper again. Alive or dead." She began to laugh in shuddering gasps. "And he's dead."

"Do you know who killed him?"

"What difference does it make?"

"Claire, listen to me. If you know anything, you must reveal it. It will help me. And your son will probably inherit a great deal of money. Tell what you know for him. For Christopher."

She looked as if a patina of stone had suddenly encased her. "Oh, God. My God. Christopher." She repeated the words again and again. Tears drenched her cheeks, but her frozen expression didn't change. She didn't make a sound. Abruptly her head fell back. She had passed out.

God, what was he going to do now? He couldn't take her back inside. Nor could he go to his apartment. He grabbed at her pouch purse and found her driver's license. It was made out to a Jean Mason. Was it an assumed name or the name and address of a friend she lived with in Glendale. In the dark, he couldn't be sure of the picture on the license.

A security policeman strolled by the line of cars. Luke pulled Claire to him, drawing her thin robe around her shoulders to conceal the glittering gold ornaments on her naked body. She lay against him limply, damply, with a cosmetic-ravaged face. He felt another surge of rage and disgust.

When the guard's footsteps had faded into silence, Luke released her and she slumped in her corner of the seat. He shoved the key in the ignition and the engine spluttered into sound. At the entrance of the parking lot, he hesitated. Which way? Where?

He shifted quietly into low gear and headed south, toward the Hollywood Freeway.

9

Claire stirred restlessly just before they reached the Torrance exit. In a hollow whisper, she asked where he was taking her. Luke thought hurriedly. If he told her and she attempted to jump out of the car, he would be unable to restrain her. He slowed speed and said cautiously that they were going to see friends. This seemed to satisfy her for a moment. Then she leaned forward tensely, inspecting the exit signs. She looked at him. Her eyes were smudged with cosmetics but they were less dazed and they were wide with fear.

"Not to the house. You're not taking me to the house!"

"No, we're not going there."

She sat back and, after a couple of miles, said in faint protest that she had a job. She had to go to work. Luke said nothing. Some job, he thought. A hundred guys, making her with their eyes.

He decided to circumvent her derelict home to avoid a possible emotional outburst and circled further south, hoping he had found the right street. He had. He pulled to the curb and switched off the motor quickly, ready to grab her if she so much as moved.

"Sara and Bob live here," she whispered.

He couldn't decide whether it was an observation or a protest. But she weakly permitted him to help her up the flagstone path. Luke hoped that Sara Brown was painting, exploring her inspirational vibes. She must have been for she answered his ring instantly. There were smudges of paint on her white smock.

"Luke Fremont! And Claire? My God! Bob," she shouted. "Wake up. We've got visitors."

Luke expelled a gusty sigh of relief. His surmise had been right. Nothing could startle Sara. She led the way to the living room as if there was nothing unusual in finding a weary, unshaven man and a partially nude young woman on her doorstep at two in the morning. Claire sank limply to a cushion, closing her eyes. Luke found he could still stand.

"I found her."

Sara snorted. "That's fairly obvious. She looks terrible. I think she could do with a drink."

"She'd better not have anything. She was drugged to the eyelashes earlier."

Sara rested her hand on Claire's forehead. "It's not drugs. She has a raging fever. Bob, hurry up!"

"Here I am. How can I work all day when I don't get any sleep at night?" He was yawning and rubbing his cropped head. When he saw Claire, he whistled. "She looks like a fugitive from a raided harem."

And that reminded Luke of his own fugitive status. He wondered if they knew about it. His legs began to tremble and he collapsed on a cushion, rubbing his stinging eyes.

"Well, just don't stand there, Bob," Sara snapped. "Help me get her to bed. Your bedroom."

Between them they half-carried, half-led Claire across the room and into the hall.

"Pour some wine, all around, Luke," Sara said. "There's a decanter on the shelf in the kitchen."

Luke filled three juice glasses and downed his at a gulp. He felt lightheaded by the time Sara and Bob returned.

"She does have a temperature," Sara announced. "Almost 102."

"She was asleep on her feet," Bob added. "Where did you pick her up, at the disco?"

Luke nodded. "Yes. And she raved about how glad she was that Jasper Dorn was dead. But when I mentioned her son, she became sort of hysterical. After that, she passed out."

106

"Who wouldn't, under the circumstances?" Sara asked. "She's really on the spot."

"What do you mean?" Luke frowned.

Sarah and Bob looked at each other, then gaped at him, and said in unison. "You mean, you don't know?"

"Know what?"

"In last night's paper. Oh, God." Sara rushed to the hall. "I spread it out on the floor in my studio. I was speckling." She returned with a crumpled armful of newspaper and thrust the front page at Luke. "Look!"

The paint-splotched headline leaped out. SISTER OF NURSING HOME DIRECTOR REVEALS DORN GRANDSON WAS INCURABLY ILL.

Luke gaped, scanning the leading paragraphs. "According to Hilda Beck, sister of L. Avery Boyd, director of the Hôtel del Sol in Belden Beach, California, Christopher Dorn, grandson of Jasper Dorn, industrialist, who was found murdered on the grounds of the nursing home Friday night, was incurably ill due to a pituitary imbalance, known as acromegaly, gigantism. Saturday night, Mr. Boyd was injured in an automobile accident which was the result of shots directed at him as he was approaching the entrance to the Hôtel's grounds. Today, Mrs. Beck said that she believed the death of Mr. Dorn and the attack on Mr. Boyd are related and she fears for her brother's life. She insisted that Mr. Dorn's murderer and her brother's assailant are the same person, someone who is avenging the child's incarceration. According to Mrs. Beck, the child escaped from the Hôtel, killing an orderly, Felix Groder. The child is presumed to have died."

There were a number of statements by endocrine specialists, describing the disastrous physical and psychological symptoms of the disease. And there were pictures. Dr. Stefan Vasa, dark, sardonic, unfriendly.

107

He stated that, at birth, Christopher had been a large but normal, healthy infant, although it was thought at the time the birth had been premature. A reproduced snapshot of the orderly, Felix Groder, shifty, small, arm in arm with Captain Leo Stone, very tall and craggy, with the prow of the *Sea Lion* in the background. A studio portrait of Claire and Gilbert Dorn, which must have been taken when they were first married.

But an artist's sketch of how Christopher Dorn might have looked, if he had lived, dominated the story. The sketch was inhuman. Or subhuman. A gnome-like figure, stooping under the weight of an enormously enlarged head, with huge hands and feet. The malformed figure had been placed in a conventional doorway, to give it human proportion, and the gnome-like impression vanished. The featureless figure became monstrous and menacing.

"Is it true, Luke?" Sara burst out. "Is it?"

He raised a haggard face. "How do I know?"

"Dr. Vasa's still protecting Claire. He didn't say anything about Gil's lie, pretending Christopher was premature so Jasper wouldn't find out that he and Claire had an affair before they were married," Sara said.

"Yeah," Bob said pointedly, "but the doctor is the only one who is protecting Claire. But the rest of the articles are slanted. J.D. and Boyd emerge like saints, J.D., hoping to spare his daughter-in-law further distress after Gil's death. And Boyd, a devoted friend. But you and Claire are on the rack. She appears to be an unnatural mother, hiding from the authorities. And you, Luke, my God, you're a wanted man!"

Sara stared through her round, rimless glasses. "You didn't kill J.D. Did you, Luke?"

"God, no."

"That's what we thought."

Luke looked up. "Is there anything in the paper about Matthew Powell?"

"It's here someplace," Bob said, rifling the sheets. "He said he didn't know anything about Christopher."

Luke told them about Powell's machinations and the money found in his files. "He wanted me to take off."

"That figures," Bob said. "If Powell was that close to J.D., he'd operate like a Borgia. You know something? I'll bet you a Harbour surfboard Claire killed J.D. She had every reason to hate that sickie."

Sara said hopefully, "Maybe when she feels better, she'll tell us."

Luke groaned. "I wonder if she's seen all this."

Sara darted into the hall and poked her head into Bob's bedroom. She closed the door. "We can't ask her now. She's sound asleep."

Luke rubbed his forehead. "Well, there's one thing, for sure. We can't stay here. We can't involve the two of you in it." He struggled to stand.

"Sit down," Sara ordered. "Didn't you come here so we could help you? Does anyone know that we know each other?"

Luke was certain he hadn't mentioned their names to Matthew Powell. "Yes, Deputy Chang in Belden Beach. But he's a great guy and he's not working on the case. Besides, he doesn't know where I am."

"Then you're safe," Sara decided. "We've been fried, grilled and toasted by hordes of detectives. There's no reason for them to come back."

Bob poured another glass of wine for Luke. "Relax, man."

But Luke couldn't relax. He felt like a fused bomb. Ready to explode. He was tensely prepared to do something. But what? How could he sit and wait for Claire to recover? Perhaps when she woke up, she wouldn't be any more lucid than she had been, in spite of Sara's diagnosis of a virus.

"You need a shave and a shower to wash off some of that fugitive-from-the-law look," Bob advised.

"And some sleep. In my bedroom. I'm going to finish my painting."

"With Claire in my bed, where am I supposed to sleep?" Bob asked grumpily.

"On the floor. You're always telling me what great discipline sleeping on the floor is." She pushed at Luke. "Go on, to the bathroom. There are extra towels in the hall linen closet."

Luke tottered into their pink and red bathroom.

Sara began to collect pillows and blankets. "Do you realize we're harboring criminals?" She looked quite happy about it.

"They're not criminals." Bob eyed his makeshift bed with distaste.

"But the police think they might be. I think we've got to get some advice. This whole thing is pretty hairy."

Bob tested his floor bed and groaned. "I was thinking the same thing. But who can we ask?"

"Whom," Sara said automatically. "I don't know. Let's think about that."

10

Chang returned from his early morning swim in time to catch the TV news. It was a repeat of what had been in the newspapers the night before, except for one development. A number of prominent citizens were requesting an investigation into nursing home policies, in general, and the Hôtel del Sol, in particular.

Hilda Beck had called twice the night before. She had apologized, deeply concerned that Chang might have been reprimanded in some way. He hadn't the heart to tell her that he had been suspended. It was only natural that she would have gone to the authorities with her brother's information. She cared for him and she wanted to protect him. But, as a result, the Hôtel del Sol certainly faced an unpleasant scrutiny. The Dorn segment on the news had ended with a telescopic scan of the chalets and the grounds, zooming in on a close-up of the armed guards and the gatehouse.

Jade, who had been watching and repeating unfamiliar words, asked, "Uncle, the newsman said that Luke was alleged to have vit. . .al information. What does alleged mean?"

"It means to assert without proof."

"Then you alleged me last night when you said I spent all of the money you gave me. I didn't." She thrust a wad of bills into his hand. "And I am showing you my new clothes. Now. Oh," she squealed. "That man at the substation—"

"Barker."

"He called while you were swimming. He wants you to call him. I'm starting to put my clothes on now." She went to her bedroom.

Chang dialed the substation. Barker was excited.

"A woman called at eight this morning. She asked to speak to you specifically and, when I told her you were on vacation, she hung up. Do you think it might have been Claire Dorn? After all, you were seen on the tube."

"No, I don't think she would call me. She'd get in touch with Powell, Dorn's executive secretary."

Barker heaved a disappointed sigh. Then, "Hold it. Something's coming in."

Chang could hear the chattering of the teletype.

Barker's excitement returned. "Two motorists turned up who say they saw a peculiar looking guy, tall and in white, running along the freeway last August. They remembered because he had such a large head. It might be the kid."

"Keep me posted," Chang said and hung up. An identification, after a year's time, was uncertain. But if it checked out, it was a confirmation of Boyd's story.

Chang eyed the phone in a kind of desperation. Why didn't Luke call?

Jade glided in and out, modeling a seemingly endless succession of sweaters and pants in every color. Chang commented distractedly and inexpertly on the intricacies of design Jade pointed out for his approval. The unidentified feminine caller, Barker had told him about, presented a challenge. There were only two women connected with the Dorn investigation. Hilda Beck and, as Luke had told him, Sara Brown. Why not? Chang asked himself. The only way to catch a fish is to cast a line. He got the Brown number in Palos Verdes from information. Sara answered on the first ring.

"This is Deputy Chang in Belden Beach. Did you try to reach me at the police station?"

Sara stammered so much, Chang couldn't understand what she was saying.

"Miss Brown, do you know where Luke Fremont is?"

"I might," she said slowly. "That is, I'd have to be sure you are acting as a friend and not a policeman."

"As a policeman, I am convinced that Luke is not involved. And, as a friend, I want to help him if I can."

"All right," Sara said decisively. "Luke told us you are a great guy. Can you come down here this afternoon?"

"Is Luke there?"

"They're both here. Luke and Claire. He turned up with her at two this morning. She's ill and he isn't in much better shape."

"Don't tell them I'm coming. They might decide to take off."

"How do you think you can help them?"

"That depends on what they can tell me."

Chang glanced at his watch. With any breaks in the traffic, he could make it by late afternoon, even in the old pickup. He didn't want to be seen in the squad car. He was taking that first step on another journey; by not informing Sheriff Mintner where Luke was, Chang was irrevocably committed.

Bob Fairway and Sara Brown must have been waiting impatiently. They fairly pulled Chang through the front door. Apparently, they had felt their secret meeting required something more than their usual Japanese robes. Sara wore a beaded jumpsuit and Bob, the inevitable jeans and studded belt. His red shirt was open to the waist.

"Are we glad to see you," he said. "Luke's in the shower, again. He said something about leaving."

"And Claire's awake but she's still in bed," Sara said. "She woke up in a snit. Didn't know where she was. Her fever's gone but she's limp as a noodle. And distrustful. She thought we were keeping her here against her will. Then she kind of gave up. Said that she didn't care what happened to her."

"Has she seen the papers or watched the news?" Chang asked.

"Not since she's been here."

"Did she say anything about her son?"

"No, except when I mentioned his name, she began to cry." Sara asked if Chang would like coffee.

He accepted it gratefully. He was troubled. A dark brown van, curtained and decaled like the ones driven by itinerant youth in search of paradise, had followed the pickup from Belden Beach to the Torrance exit. It might be that Sheriff Mintner had put a tail on Chang, hoping it would lead to Luke. But then it could also be attributed to the sinister forces that, Chang now felt, originated, in some unknown way, with Matthew Powell. The incident had filled Chang with a sense of urgency he didn't like. It was the apprehensive feeling authority, legal or illegal, was relentlessly closing in, a sensation that he, always before on the side of law and order, had never known. He had driven haphazardly around Palos Verdes for some time before pulling up at the indicated address.

Sara thrust a steaming mug of coffee in his hand. "Anything else?"

"I'd like to speak to Luke, first."

She pointed toward a doorway in the hall. "Go on in. He should be out of the shower in a second. I'll get Claire up."

Chang entered the steamy bathroom and sat down on the edge of the tub, just as the door to the stall shower opened. Luke stared. It was the look of a man who has been betrayed by every friend. "I might have known it," he said bitterly, grabbing up a towel. "Bob or Sara called you. Right?"

114

"Don't be such a damn fool," Chang said heatedly. "I didn't drive all the way down here to arrest you. The LAPD would have sent a helicopter if I'd reported where you were. Do you know about Christopher and the nursing home?"

"Yes."

"How about Claire Dorn?"

"How should I know. She wasn't making much sense last night." Luke slammed his fist against the basin. "I wish I'd never gone looking for her, for all the good it did."

"Boyd thinks she had Dorn killed and is out to get him. It was the only part of Boyd's story Hilda didn't tell the police."

"My God!" Luke stared.

"If Claire tells what she knows, it would certainly clear you."

"And implicate herself? No way."

"We've got to make her talk."

Luke was all for storming into the bedroom and confronting Claire that moment. Chang managed to restrain him. "Since Boyd destroyed all records of the child's tests and treatment, she can deny the child was a patient which eliminates any motive she might have."

"Chang, I think Boyd is lying. The whole thing is too weird."

"Why would he lie? He is terrified. And he admits to the cover-up about Groder's death. Give me a chance to feel Claire out. Just tell me quickly where you found her."

Luke described the disco and her sex goddess dance. "But I learned nothing. Sara thinks she had a virus of some kind. But she could have been tripped out of her skull on drugs. Before she passed out, she kept saying how glad she was that her father-in-law was dead. She meant that, all right."

115

"That fits with what Boyd told me. Get your clothes on." Luke was still in shorts. "She's probably badly frightened."

Luke pulled a T-shirt over his head. "She could turn me in and get you into trouble."

"I'm not in uniform and, if I were, I'd be masquerading. I've been suspended."

"Why!"

"For a number of reasons. I telephoned Powell, defending you. I've been guilty of dereliction of duty in not passing on Boyd's information the minute I heard it. And Sheriff Mintner has been led to believe that the plant I sent you had a sexual motive."

"Who put that out? Matthew Powell?"

"It looks that way."

"God, what's going on? I think he put that money in my files because he wanted me on the run. Why?"

"Come on. Let's see if Claire can cast some illumination."

She was curled up on one of the water cushions. Her feet were bare and she was wearing cut-off jeans and a blue sweater belonging to Sara who was bustling about with sandwiches and coffee. Luke introduced Chang.

Claire looked across the room with hostility. "Aren't you Deputy Chang from Belden Beach? I heard on television that you weren't investigating my father-in-law's murder."

"I'm not here in an official capacity."

Sara said explosively. "Claire, we're trying to help you. Haven't you heard the news?" She held out a sheaf of crumpled newspaper clippings.

Claire took a careful bite of her sandwich. "Of course, I have. Mr. Boyd's story is a complete lie."

A stunned silence filled the room.

Chang recovered first. "You mean, your son was never a patient in the Hôtel del Sol?"

116

"No. After Gil's death, Christopher and I moved to my father-in-law's house in the Valley. My son was never very well. He died and he was cremated and buried in the Dorn family plot. It was a private funeral, only the two of us."

"Why haven't you reported this to the authorities?" Chang asked.

"Should I have?" She paused and looked down at her hands. "With both Christopher and Gil gone, I wanted to get as far away from the Dorn orbit as I possibly could. I changed my name and took the job at the disco eventually, because I like to dance. Besides, I knew he could never find me there."

Was it true? Chang wondered. Or had Dorn arranged this, too? He studied her. She was so unresponsive. What on earth would move her. A threat? A plea to maternal pity?

Luke was studying her, too. She no longer looked like a sex goddess. Her face was scrubbed and wan, dark hair pulled back severely. Luke wished that Chang had seen her as he had the night before, her nude body and her face a mask of sexual frenzy. If Chang had, he wouldn't have been so gentle or courteous with her. Luke wanted to force her out of her hostile indifference.

Apparently, Bob felt the same way. "Come off it, Claire. Are you asking us to believe that you and Christopher lived with J.D.? You couldn't stand the guy."

"Gil's death changed all that."

Chang asked a number of questions about Gil's death and Claire answered them unemotionally and factually. He had tripped over a terrace chair and fallen to the shore below.

Chang asked bluntly, "Where were you the night Jasper Dorn was killed?"

She looked at him defiantly. "I was at home. I guess this virus was coming on."

117

"You said last night that you were glad your father-in-law was dead," Luke said.

"Many people didn't like him. And I'm sure they are pleased he's no longer around."

"Including you," Sara said.

"Yes, including me." Claire glared at Luke. "You're the number one boy scout for Dorn Enterprises. Explain why you brought me here and why I'm being questioned this way."

Luke felt his face go red. Boy scout! "You were ill last night and I brought you to friends. We want to help you."

"Help me or help yourself? You could have called the police, but you didn't, because you would be arrested."

"Damn it—" Luke began.

Chang interrupted, narrowing his eyes. And he played his trump card. "Mrs. Dorn, or do you prefer, Jean Mason? You have been lying. Your son was seen after he escaped from the nursing home. Two motorists have reported that last August an individual, wearing a white shirt and trousers, was running rapidly along the freeway. It is hardly a suitable place for jogging. It was dusk and their descriptions were vague, but both of them recalled the figure looked deformed due to an overlarge head."

For the second time that afternoon the room crashed into stunned silence.

Four pairs of eyes focussed on Claire, and even Luke, as critical as he was of her, felt sympathy. A most terrible look of yearning, dwindling into distrust crossed her face.

"I don't believe you," she choked out.

"The sergeant at the Belden Beach substation got it over the teletype, just before I left for Palos Verdes. You were told that your son escaped and died. Have you even wondered if he might still be alive?"

Claire seemed to collapse in on herself, as if a large

118

invisible fist were bearing down, crushing her. Vivid color stained her cheeks.

"Lies!" she burst out. "It's all lies. I can prove Christopher is buried in the Dorn family plot!"

Sara said sagely, "I'll bet J.D. arranged that. It's the kind of thing he'd do."

Claire looked defiantly at Chang. "And you can't prove that my son was a patient in the nursing home."

"How do you know that?" Chang asked quickly.

"Because there are no records. . .because he wasn't there."

"Oh, no!" Luke said harshly. "You know there are no records because you were told they were destroyed."

Bob said, "We don't seem to be getting anywhere fast. Let's start over."

Claire stood. The lassitude from her questionable virus and her emotional turmoil had completely disappeared. She even smiled frigidly. "There's no reason to start over. It's finished. Ended. And since that is *my* car outside. I'm leaving. My keys," she told Luke, holding out her hand.

Sara protested that she wasn't well enough to leave. Luke, in consternation, looked at Chang who nodded slightly. Luke tossed the key ring to her.

"You might remember," she said, "no one knows where I live and where I work. But if the police learn I'm Jean Mason, I'll know one of you told, and I'll tell them about this. . .interesting talk today and you'll all end up in jail. Boy Scout is suspected of something."

She walked out the front door and a moment later drove away.

"Wow," Bob said, "she has changed and then some."

"I told you she was gutsy," Sara added speculatively. "Say, maybe she helped Christopher escape and they planned J.D.'s death together."

"Miss Brown," Chang said. "You show quite a talent for intrigue. But, no. Having learned her son was seen, alive, has raised a desperate hope that he might still be alive. She is protecting him."

"Why?" Sara asked.

"Christopher killed a man. That orderly, Groder."

"For God's sake," Luke shouted. "On the vague identification of a couple of motorists, you people seem to believe that a deformed and incurably ill boy is alive! It probably happened just as Boyd told it. And Claire is lying to protect herself. She had reason enough to hate both Boyd and Dorn. She's protecting herself."

"I'd better remove the boy scout here to a place where he can cool off," Chang said, standing.

"But we don't know everything," Sara cried. "Why did someone shoot at Luke and who tried to blow up his car?"

"I'm not sure," Chang said.

But Sara would not be deterred. "Maybe it's connected with that Mr. Powell who put the money in Luke's safe."

"Sara," Bob said firmly, exerting authority for once, "the less we know, the better. We won't tell anyone you've been here. And since we don't know where you're going, we can't tell that either."

Chang departed formally, thanking them for their help and promising they would be told everything as soon as possible. The men went out to the pickup.

"Would you take my advice, Luke, and turn yourself in?"

"No. . .and where are we going?"

Chang sighed. "If I'm not in my greenhouse, as usual, Sheriff Mintner might suspect something. I don't want to be questioned. We're going to Belden Beach."

"Then why are we headed in the opposite direction?"

120

"I'm fairly certain I was followed down here today. A dark brown Chevy van. If it were Mintner's doing, we'd probably be arrested by now. So it must be connected with the attempts on your life. He probably lost you when you tore out of the Dorn Building yesterday morning, and he figured he might pick up your trail through me."

"God, I almost wish I'd stayed in Powell's office. I'd be safe in jail by now."

"Say the word and I'll drive you there."

"I'll be damned if I will. Powell's probably got a few more tricks to play."

"The deck is loaded, for sure. That columnist Digby must be right. Survival Kit is a multimillion dollar hoax."

"And Powell is in it up to his ears. Maybe I'd better get in touch with Digby. See what he knows."

"Could be." Chang had circled around to the freeway south of Palos Verdes and, when he approached an on-ramp, there was no sign of the brown van. The pickup joined the stream of traffic.

"And talking to Claire was a waste of time," Luke burst out. "Do you think she's involved?"

"No. And I think our talk was most revealing. Her intense emotional reaction to the possibility that her son might be alive was most revealing. There are a number of interpretations."

"You don't deny she was lying, every damn word?"

"That's true. But there are three possible reasons. One, if she is behind a plot to kill Dorn and Boyd, then, as you said, she is protecting herself. Two, her abrupt change of identity and life style, even the psuedo burial of her son could have been arranged by Dorn, implemented by threats which still exist."

"Powell?"

"It's possible. But the third, which I prefer, is that she is possessed with hope that her son may be alive.

121

If we could prove Christopher was a patient in the Hôtel, she would probably tell us what really happened. . .Luke, I think I've got it. The boy's books. Boyd returned them to her. There might be some inscription, a Hôtel stamp and notation of ownership. They're probably in her apartment."

"She might have destroyed them."

"Wouldn't she treasure his only possessions?"

Luke laughted bitterly. "I can just see us, ringing the doorbell and asking to get a look at them."

"Give the problem some creative thought."

Luke lapsed into an uneasy silence. Sometime later, Chang said musingly, "I wonder what the boy did after he escaped."

"He hid someplace. Probably died. What else could he have done? Looking the way he did and unable to talk."

"But lack of speech doesn't necessarily mean lack of intelligence. The doctors couldn't test the extent of his comprehension. He might have learned a great deal from television. And the books Claire sent him. After all, he planned an escape, killed Groder and outwitted the guards."

"Chang," Luke said in rising hope, "what about that hut out at the commune, all those chains? Lily was lying when she told us she didn't know why Kelso built it."

"You're right! I'll drive out there tomorrow," Chang said. He should have thought of it sooner. "And the commune might not be a bad place for you to stay for a few days." Luke looked the part, unshaven and crumpled. Lily could be counted on to help, although that brute, Kelso, might cause trouble.

They had reached the turn-off to Belden Beach. Chang drove slowly, looking for any indication that Mintner might be there. But the sleepy town looked normal and there was no brown van in sight.

Luke, slumped low in the seat, said, "You've done

enough. I'd better get lost someplace.''

''Take it easy. Go on into the greenhouse. I'll check with the substation, see what the latest is, and check with Jade if there have been any calls today.''

Luke slipped away into the humid darkness.

Chang found Jade, holding the telephone. ''It's for you. A young woman. She called sooner.''

''Before,'' Chang said automatically, as he grabbed the phone. ''Yes?''

''This is Jean Mason.''

Chang's spirits lifted. Claire Dorn, and she had learned all the strategy involved in a change of identity. Her voice was impersonal.

''The information you wanted earlier today is available now. I need to consult your friend. Is he there?''

Chang wondered if it was a trick to implicate Luke in some way. ''I can get in touch with him.''

''His advice is truly needed. A young person is involved. Can you ask him to come to my apartment?''

''I can ask him but he may not wish to.'' Chang had all but decided that her request was too extraordinary to be taken seriously. But with her next statement, he changed his mind.

''I lied to you today because I was forced to by a very evil man.''

Chang glanced at his watch. ''You can expect our friend around six.'' He hung up and went out to the greenhouse. Luke was lurking behind the mass of plants ready for delivery to Los Angeles. Chang looked so alert and confident, Luke asked apprehensively what had happened.

''Claire called. She admitted that she lied this afternoon because of Dorn. She wants you to go to her apartment. It concerns her son.''

''No way. That gal is trouble. Period.''

''You may learn something that will clear you of the false charges and implicate Powell. It may even solve Dorn's murder.''

123

"I don't trust her."

"But you'll be safe at her place."

"And just how would I get to Glendale?"

"In the pickup. You can drop my delivery at my cousin's shop on the way. Here, help me load the truck."

With reluctance Luke finally agreed to go and began to collect the plants. Since his original fifty dollars had dwindled to half that amount, Chang handed over a wad of bills. "You'd better stay off the freeways. Take the secondary roads."

Luke pocketed the money. "I have a feeling we're both at the end of that well-known limb, and some-one's already chopping it down."

"Perhaps. But the tenacity of a tree to produce an-other branch is a natural phenomenon. Yet so pre-dictable that the miracle of its activity is not perceived."

"I don't know what you're talking about."

"Business, as usual. Per schedule, early morning I will be plunging in the Pacific Ocean. Aha! And the pickup is not behind the greenhouse. Yes, the delivery of plants has arrived at the garden shop. No, Chang has not been seen around Belden Beach all day. Only Jade, who has been monitoring the telephone, knows that he had been sitting in his study, waiting for a call from Jean Mason to say that the advice she received is satisfactory. And so and so steps will be taken."

Luke had to laugh. "Chang, sometimes you act as if you were five years old. Or maybe a hundred and five."

Chang grinned. "Since I am midway between that span, my paltry wisdom dictates that I give you the address of the garden shop. He begins work at dawn so he will be there. And, Luke, you'll be safe from arrest at Claire's. But not necessarily from the person who tried to kill you."

"As if I could forget it," Luke said and stomped out to the truck.

11

Chang watched the pickup disappear around a corner of the block, waiting a few moments. But no brown van passed by. He slept a few restless hours and, when he heard the thud of the paper against the front door, he gave up and went out to collect it. The press had made the best, or the worst, of the motorists' identification of Christopher Dorn.

MANIAC ON THE LOOSE. HAVE YOU SEEN THE FREAK?

Artists had produced a menacing figure which was a combination of every fictional monster from Frankenstein's creation to Hiroshima's atomic mutants.

Several eminent endocrinologists suggested that the boy-man could have survived for a limited time. A famous doctor from Harvard Medical School described in detail the physical and psychological deformations of acromegaly. "The normal development of familial, environmental and educated curbs to psychopathic behavior would be completely lacking. The subject, functioning wholly with his limbic brain, the seat of man's most primitive intellectual capacities which is restricted to instinctual behavior—flight, fight, food and sex—should be considered exceedingly dangerous. Any threat to sources of food, freedom and sex would engender primal rage and predisposition to violence."

Matthew Powell continued to deny all knowledge of the child's condition, but stated that official efforts to find the fugitives, Claire Dorn and Luke Fremont, were grossly inadequate.

L. Avery Boyd would be charged with criminal negligence, for having failed to prevent the boy's escape, as soon as he was well enough to appear in court.

Many civic and church organizations were demanding investigation of agencies responsible for the safety of the public.

"What does it all mean, Uncle?" Jade's serene face was furrowed and uneasy.

"It's a phenomenon known in this country as investigative journalism. Will you hold breakfast? I need a swim."

He jogged down to the beach. He had never been able to decide whether it was the chilly water or the discipline of stroking around the length of the pier that always clarified his thoughts.

He was beginning to perceive that the murder of Jasper Dorn was not an isolated act of the taking of a single life. His death resembled the planting of a voracious and evil seed. Each shoot that appeared was related, yet developed in a malignant fashion. What the full flowering would bring, could not be envisioned, except that its destructive force was unquestionable. He plunged into the chilly water.

He had breasted several crashing waves and was stroking steadily toward the *Sea Lion* when he heard young voices and a barking dog, kids playing on the derelict sloop again. Treading water, he called out and shortly a number of guilty faces ringed the rail, looking down at him.

"I warned you," Chang shouted breathlessly. "I'm going to tell Sergeant Barker to call your parents and—"

A tousled-headed boy shouted, "Someone's been on the boat. The deck hardly slants, at all."

Chang saw that the sloop rose almost parallel with the sea and oily bilge water eddied around the hull like green-black scum. Someone must have been pumping out the hold.

"Okay, kids, listen—" he began. But they were

126

already halfway down the pier, racing toward the shore.

Swimming in a wide arc to avoid the scum, Chang rounded the end of the pier and, decidedly out of breath, reached the beach. He stared back at the sloop. If Leo Stone's brother had arranged with a salvage company to pump out the *Sea Lion*, there would have been electrical equipment on the pier. The sloop's electrical system had blown out with the explosion.

Chang's mind wandered to the previous Saturday afternoon in front of the police station when he had told Luke that the only man he knew who would have had the strength to carry Jasper Dorn was Captain Leo Stone.

Chang toweled his shoulders and began to walk slowly toward home. And Leo Stone, before his supposed death, had been right in thinking that Groder had died up at the Hôtel.

Chang's step quickened. Was it possible that Groder had learned who Christopher Dorn was by contriving that leak in Boyd's office, taking copies of the boy's files and showing them to Stone? Later, Stone, angry and sorrowing over Groder's death, would have presented a serious threat to Jasper Dorn and his web of concealment about his grandson. According to Luke, Dorn had been paying blackmail, as revealed by Powell. Dorn was not a man to permit such a threat to continue. He might have arranged for the sloop's engines to explode. And the body, half eaten by sharks, had been erroneously identified. Stone, alive, might have killed Dorn to avenge Groder's death as well as the attempt on his own life. And if Stone were alive, wouldn't he try to salvage his beloved *Sea Lion*?

Chang decided that he would board the sloop that night, after dark, and conceal himself somewhere below deck. Whoever the intruder was, he had come and gone furtively, and he would return.

12

"What made you decide to trust Dorn Enterprises' number one boy scout?" Luke asked Claire suspiciously.

"I'm not sure I do trust you. But we seem to be in the same position."

Luke agreed wearily. A half dozen times on the time-consuming secondary roads, he was tempted to say to hell with it and head for the freeway. But Chang's caution had deterred him. And taking a tip from the way Chang had inspected the streets in Belden Beach, Luke had driven around the area where Claire's apartment was located. He had then parked several blocks to the north, eyeing cars furtively, ducking behind a massive palm tree when a brown van idled by. Luke couldn't be sure it was the van Chang had seen, but he was swept with a sick fear that it might be.

Claire's apartment was a replica of his own, a sleepy, indifferent doorman, monitoring a closed circuit TV system which made you feel as safe as if you were living in a treehouse in the middle of a jungle.

It was almost six when he had arrived; only a few people were in the lobby, and Luke was admitted without any difficulty. He had used the name, Percy, again. And, like his own place, Claire's studio apartment was indifferently furnished in motel decor.

"And I realized," Claire said aggressively, "you are the one person who can help me. Have you heard the news this morning?"

"No."

"What Chang said yesterday about Christopher being seen on the freeway seems to be true. That's why I need your—your advice."

"My advice to you is to tell whatever you know to the police and anyone else who'll listen."

"Thanks for nothing. I've already come to that conclusion." She hesitated. "Luke, please, I must tell you. And only you." She fell silent, filling their coffee cups.

Luke eyed her warily. How many of her swings of mood had he seen? From hysteria, to maudlin sorrow, to hostile indifference to the present pretense of friendship. What was she leading up to?

She was still wearing the cutt-off jeans and T-shirt belonging to Sara Brown. But she had brushed her hair and used pale lipstick. Even perfume. If she intended to employ feminine influence, she couldn't have picked on a less responsive guy. She was another Lori of the world. Only worse. She was more intelligent and, like a chameleon, she could change moods and emotions, at will.

"It's all true," she said abruptly. "Christopher was a patient in the Hôtel del Sol."

Luke groaned. "Why didn't you say so yesterday afternoon in Palos Verdes?"

"There are so many reasons, I—I don't know where to begin." She rubbed her forehead. "I have blamed myself a thousand times. But Jasper tricked me. I should have known how he operated. Gil warned me often enough. But Jasper said that Christopher would have the best care there and whatever treatment or operation that was necessary to cure him."

"According to Boyd, everything was done, but nothing was effective."

"Are you sure?"

"You mean to say you didn't know?"

"No. Once Christopher was committed Jasper told me my silence was the price I would pay for the expensive tests and treatment. No one was to know where my son was. Or why. I was not permitted any visits with him. And I was to get lost. So I became Jean Mason. Jasper arranged it. The job dancing in the disco was my idea. I needed the money and I knew Jasper would never think of looking for me there. I was afraid. So afraid.''

''You could have reported all this, gotten legal advice.''

She jumped to her feet. And now she was angry. ''I couldn't be sure Jasper was telling the truth, about my son's escape and death. He arranged for the false burial in the event someone might begin to wonder where Christopher was. Don't you see? He might have had my son moved someplace else. I hoped he had. It would mean that my son wasn't dead. That's why I did everything that evil man told me to. For my son.''

''But after Dorn was killed, you could have asked for advice and help.''

''Why! I felt I couldn't endure being followed, questioned, hounded by reporters. It was horrible enough when Gil died. It was ancient history. All I had left were those.'' She pointed to the dinette table and a pile of picture books. ''Don't you believe me?''

''I don't know.'' Luke felt a surge of hope. At least, his trip wasn't a complete failure. He wondered how he could contrive to look at them. He managed to look no more than politely interested when she crossed the room unsteadily and returned with a faded, smudged atlas.

''Look. When I got home last night, I leafed through them again. I often do. And I found this.'' Her hands shook so violently, he could scarcely focus on the pages. ''Highway maps are missing. California, Nevada, Idaho and Montana.'' She clutched the atlas convulsively. ''I think Christopher is alive!''

Her wide dark eyes looked sick, feverishly full of irrational hope. ''I know Christopher is alive. He escaped and took the maps so he could find his way to Silverleaf.''

"That's impossible! He was incurably ill.''

"No," her voice rose. "He's alive and he went to Silverleaf where he was born.''

"How could he have known where he was born?''

She swallowed with difficulty, and her words spilled out. "When he was about a month old, I realized he could understand what people said. He reacted emotionally, curiosity, humor, pleasure in the foods he liked. There was his physical development and strength. He could walk at six weeks although I didn't know it at first. But he knew it wasn't normal, so he'd roam about at night. Milk spilled in the kitchen, records broken, his toys moved. He never did these things when Gil was around because he was afraid. He knew Gil hated him. And so he would pretend to be a normal baby. Don't you see? He was protecting himself.''

Claire was in such an agitated state that Luke wondered what might calm her. A stiff drink? He might even have to slap her face or shake her. "Calm down, Claire. Your voice is—''

She hadn't heard him. "I intend to go to Silverleaf. Christopher might have been there. He might be there now. But I don't feel up to it. I can't make it alone. I've got to have help. You.''

Luke felt himself go cold.

She collapsed in a chair and pressed her hands to her face. Her lips were trembling, but her eyes were watching him acutely. He considered several ways to point out the futility of her idea, but it must be approached with logic, even though it was as illogical as anything he had ever heard.

"You'd have a better chance of making it without me. No one knows you as Jean Mason.''

"There's no way to fly there directly. Someone must help drive.''

"But I'm in a hell of a spot. And I don't have any money. Not enough."

She drew a savings account bank book from the hip pocket of the cut-offs and tossed it to him. It belonged to Jean Mason and she was a wealthy woman. "Jasper's way of easing his nonexistent conscience," she said bitterly. "I never intended to use it. Now I'm glad it's there."

Luke tried another approach. "How do you intend to find your son? Explore the village? The forest?"

"Of course not. I'm going to see Dr. Vasa."

Dr. Stefan Vasa. Luke remembered him from the television interview, an erudite, somber man and certainly not a backwoods G.P. "Wouldn't it be simpler to telephone him?"

"I already have. Twice. He was out both times and didn't return my calls. Stefan is not an ordinary person. He values his peace and privacy. That's why he lives in Silverleaf. But once I have explained that there would be no publicity, he'd do anything to help me."

That was true, Luke thought, according to Sara Brown. The doctor had been very protective of Claire. Obviously, she had thought up all the answers and finally Luke exploded. "Listen. Your son was incurably ill. He was deformed. He couldn't talk. And he would have deteriorated mentally and physically. It's not possible that he's alive."

"But it is," she flared. "Except for the way he looked, he was strong and healthy."

"At first, perhaps. But not later. We're not going."

"Yes, we are." Her face hardened. "If you don't go with me, I'll call Matthew Powell and the police. The only way you got here was in that pickup belonging to your friend, Chang. You're as good as in jail, right now."

"You'll lose the protection of your false identity."

"What difference does that make?"

God! Luke felt trapped. It was futile to blame Chang, whose urging had plunged him in the center of a lousy complication he could have lived without forever. He couldn't think of a single way to outmaneuver her. And then it occurred to him how highly she had spoken of Dr. Vasa. She trusted him. Certainly, the doctor would grasp how unstable she was. Perhaps, he would insist on medical or psychiatric treatment. And that would free Luke from this hideously unwelcome alliance. And a side benefit existed, too. Silverleaf was remote and isolated. What better place could he find to hide for a few days?

Suddenly and uneasily, Luke remembered the sketch of what the boy might have become if he had survived. Immense. The features of the grotesquely large head twisted into a subhuman snarl of hatred. Hands and arms thrust menacingly forward, legs wide apart, the misshapen feet.

"Claire," he said gently, "if your son is alive, it might be better if he were never found. He would be so. . .changed, it might destroy you."

"No horror could equal what I've lived through for almost five years, thinking that he would believe I deserted him willingly. I must find him and tell him that everything I did was because I love him."

In a last desperate move, Luke opened the cover of the atlas. The first two pages had been carefully cut out. Whatever had been written on them was lost forever. He was certain all the other books had been similarly divested of proof that Christopher was a patient in the Hôtel del Sol.

"All right," he said wearily. "We've got to plan how to get there without being followed." He leafed through the atlas and found a map of the West Coast. "The best plan would be to fly to some city not too far from Silverleaf. Then hire a car and drive the rest of the way."

While Luke studied the map, Claire was strangely silent. When he looked up, she was smiling, relaxed, easy. "I knew it would work out. It's perfect. Even to the way you look. No one would ever know that you're Luke Fremont."

"Some one does. Someone has tried to kill me twice. You might be included in the third try." She, at least, had sense enough to look frightened. "And now, Jean Mason, I have a condition. I must telephone Chang and tell him where we're going." He might have known she would have the last word.

She smiled again. "Of course, but it would be better if you called him after we are safely on the way."

Luke called Chang from the Tacoma, Washington, airport.

13

Chang shifted position numbly, stretching his cramped knees as best he could. He was huddled in a narrow storage closet, off the main galley of the *Sea Lion*. The closet was empty, except for a pair of foul-smelling plastic slickers and some mis-matched rubber boots. Whatever else it had contained, had probably been taken by local pier fishermen or the children.

He had boarded the sloop just after sunset when the pier fishermen had departed. In the dim light, the sloop was riding higher in the water and the steep list to the sea side was less canted. More oily bilge water lapped at the hull. Someone had been using a hand pump, although a search below decks had not revealed any kind of equipment. Chang hoped that it was Leo Stone.

The storage closet with its slatted doors gave Chang a comprehensive area to watch, part of the galley on the right and, beyond that, the entrance to the engine cubicle which was a tangle of rusted steel cable and unidentifiable flotsam, floating in the murky sump water.

The hull of the *Sea Lion* rose and fell with the ocean current and the stern wash from the passing of small craft. Between the incessant motion and the fishy odors and scurry of rats, Chang fervently wished his vigil would not last long. He checked his watch in a brief gleam of his flashlight. It was almost nine o'clock.

Chang snapped off the flashlight and sat back in darkness. Claire and Luke were nearing Silverleaf. Luke's brief call from Tacoma, Washington, had considerably increased Chang's sense of urgency. It was to be expected that Claire, given the possibility that her son was alive, would grasp at the slightest clue as to where he might have gone. But Luke had told him he had spotted a brown van near Claire's apartment. Chang told himself there must be hundreds of brown vans. But it accomplished nothing.

He heard the cough of another outboard motor and tensed. All of the small craft that had passed by had chugged away into silence. But this motor cut off abruptly and there was a wash of oars. Someone was rowing toward the sloop. A moment later, there was a thump on deck, and muted, irregular footsteps could be heard. There was another series of thuds, as if equipment were being taken aboard. Chang leaned forward, eyes staring intently through an open slat.

In the semi-light from the hatchway, a tall figure could be indistinctly seen. He wore a short seaman's jacket and trousers of some drab color and rubber-soled sneakers. The shoulders were broad and powerful. He was methodically moving objects, some of them heavy, through the hatchway and down the laddered steps. He moved with difficulty. One of his legs seemed disabled. In the galley, he rested for a moment. Chang could hear his labored breathing. Then limping, he began to move the equipment into the engine room. Only his back could be seen.

Chang risked opening the door a fraction of an inch when the wide beam of a stationary flash illuminated the area. He widened the fraction when he heard the rhythmic pound of the pump.

He debated what to do. From all indications the pumping activity would continue for hours, and Chang did not intend to sit in the closet half the night. Finally he left the closet quietly and crept to the far end of the galley. His foot struck a metal hook used to secure the bottom of a door. The rhythmic sounds ceased. The stranger uttered a hoarse growling sound, head cocked to one side. Then he grunted and began working again. Chang risked another few steps.

Hunched over, the man looked huge. The muscles of his broad back, tensing with movement.

136

"Stone," Chang called out. "Stone, is that you?"

The man rose to his feet and whirled. Chang had a glimpse of the face, eyes and teeth gleaming whitely in a face distorted by smears of black grease. He leaped forward, raising a wrench. "Damn you, Chang!"

"Stone—" Chang hit the floor like a sack of peat moss.

When he came to, he was stretched out on one of the bunks. Blinking, he realized that the wide-beamed flash was now in the galley. Expecting to be tied up, he found that he was free, and he pushed up weakly. He fingered a crusted swelling behind his right ear and swallowed, resisting nausea.

A large, wide shadow loomed over him. "Here, drink this."

Chang took the flask and swallowed, gasping. He was able to bring Stone's face into focus. Stone had removed his visored cap and some of the grease had been wiped away, but his eyes were hard, squinting with anger. When Chang looked toward the hatchway, Stone moved so that he stood between it and the bunk.

"I hit you too hard. But you took me by surprise. Goddam it, Chang, why did you have to come nosing around?"

"Because," Chang said weakly, "I suspected who murdered Jasper Dorn and I guess I've found him."

"That son of a bitch," Stone muttered. He uttered a disgusted sound deep in his throat.

Chang took another gulp. He was beginning to feel better. He didn't expect Stone to show any mercy but, if he could encourage Stone to talk, it might give him the advantage of time. And he would have the satisfaction of confirming his suspicions. "How did it happen? Did Groder tell you about the Dorn grandson in the Hôtel?"

Stone slammed his fists together. "Right. Groder stole some of the kid's records when he fixed it so

137

Boyd's toilet would spring a leak. Groder was smart. Not like me. He figured out the code they were in. Groder worked out a hell of a good blackmail idea. Then he gets himself killed. On the beach?" Stone laughed harshly. "I told you Groder would never walk on the beach. Now I read that the Dorn kid did it. But that son of a bitch Dorn makes it look like a mugging. Plunks him down like a dead fish on the beach." Stone rubbed his grease-blackened face; his voice was harsh, uneven. "Jesus, poor Groder."

Chang slid off the bunk. He was surprised he could stand.

"Get back up there," Stone rasped.

Chang fell back against the bunk. "So you went ahead with the blackmail idea?"

"Right. And it worked. More than the money, it used to give me a real kick to see Dorn's mad face. But I kept it up too long. Dorn works out how to kill me. Blow up the *Sea Lion*. But he didn't kill me. No, by God, not me."

Limping, Stone began to pace the galley, ducking at the overhead beams. Every now and then he rubbed his crippled leg.

"What did you do after the explosion? Swim ashore?"

"Yeah. I know every inch of the coast and every shack on it. By the time I could walk again, I had it all figured out in my mind. I decided to give the bastard time to think I was dead. Then I called his nigger secretary, with the signal we used when it was time to get it up with the money. . .would you please tell Mr. Dorn that the shipment of some crap—we kept changing the crap—is ready? That meant we were to meet near the Costa Marina. That last time I called him, he was in Washington and was he ever shook." Stone laughed again. "He thought I was dead."

"So you arranged a final meeting?"

138

"Right. And the son of a bitch was already dead when I got there."

Chang stared in disbelief. "You're lying."

"I sure as hell am not! He was dead, I tell you. Blood all over the car. His face looked like it went through a meat grinder. I wouldn't have killed him that way. I would of broken his neck. I was shook. But then I got an idea. Groder would have gone for it. I moved him in his car up to the nursing home so that bastard Boyd would have some explaining to do. And I drove the car back to the Marina. Got in my outboard and left."

Chang insisted Stone repeat the story several times. It was Dorn's Washington itinerary that convinced Chang that Stone was telling the truth. He had found the itinerary on the sand, behind the car, and had shoved it in Dorn's jacket pocket so he could be easily identified.

"Did you shoot at Boyd by the gatehouse?"

"Jesus, no. Boyd's in for trouble, already. And I had money and I was supposed to be dead. I decided to pump out the *Sea Lion*. . .Jesus, why did you have to come nosing around?. . .and go on down to Mexico, somewhere along the coast. And she was almost ready."

Stone sat down on a bench as if someone had hit him hard in the stomach. He hunched forward, holding his head in his hands. "That's what Groder and me were going to do. Go to Mexico. God!"

"You'd better tell Sheriff Mintner what happened. You'll live the rest of your life worrying about being found out."

"I don't give a damn. Nobody's going to find me. I've got plans." There was a return of Stone's belligerency. "The point is, what are you going to do about it?"

Chang frowned. In a few days' time, he had completely reversed the disciplines that had guided his life. Stone was guilty of blackmail and he was an accessory to murder. But Dorn was guilty of infinitely greater crimes. And they had been committed, not out of passion, but in the frigid emotion of selfish manipulation, of self-interest. Chang sighed. "I'm not going to do anything about it, Leo. Get back to pumping."

"You mean it?"

"Yes."

Stone tried to say something and failed. He scooped up the flash and returned to the engine room.

On unsteady legs, Chang reached the hatchway and, on the pier, headed for shore. If Stone hadn't killed Dorn, who had? It now seemed certain that the murder had been a first act in a sinister scenario to discredit and destroy Luke Fremont. And it all pointed to Matthew Powell. The urgency Chang felt was unbearable. Claire was in danger, too. Powell's agents probably had followed them and could be in Silverleaf now.

Chang's thoughts were as gloomy and dark as his home looked when he rounded the corner of the street. He felt a throb of apprehension. Jade should be awake, watching one of her interminable TV programs.

His footsteps rang sharply on the narrow porch. He tried the door; it had been bolted from the inside. He called, "Jade! Jade, are you there?"

He heard her voice faintly. "Uncle Chang?"

"Yes. Open up."

She struggled with the bolt. The door flew open and she fell against him. She was sobbing, stammering an explanation. "Someone—in the greenhouse. Smashing—crashing. We didn't know what—"

"We! Who's here with you?"

"I am." It was a voice from the corner of the dark room. "Lily. I left the commune this afternoon."

By this time, Chang had switched on the overhead light. Lily wore her usual halter and long untidy skirt;

her bulging backpack lay on the floor near the couch. She had a black eye. Jade in a short shift was rubbing an ugly bruise on her right shin. The girls' faces were white with fear.

"Now," Chang said, "tell me all over again. And slowly."

It seemed that Lily had arrived around eight and, at Jade's urging, had decided to wait for Chang to return. Around ten, the noises had begun in the greenhouse, and the girls had locked the doors and windows and turned off all the lights. Then the intruder had prowled around the house for some time. After he had left, they were too frightened to move and had waited in the dark.

Lily fingered her black eye gingerly. "I think it was Kelso, Chang. We had a fight before I left."

Grabbing up his service revolver, Chang told them to bolt the door behind him and went out to the greenhouse, switching on lights. He groaned. " 'To be tattered, is to be renewed,' " he told himself. But it was scant comfort.

The greenhouse was a shambles. There was a knee-high pile of rubble on the floor. Pots were smashed; dead and dying plants were crushed and trampled. The tall azalea trees had been axed off at the roots. Panes of glass were cracked or gaped blackly against the starless sky.

Chang moved swiftly.

In the house, he told Jade to pack up her new clothes. "I'm calling our cousin to come get both of you. You can stay with his family. It isn't safe here." Jade went immediately to her bedroom.

Lily sat dejectedly while Chang attended to her black eye. "I'm sorry, Chang. I should have known Kelso would follow me."

"We won't worry about that now. Why did you want to see me?"

Lily winced. "The pest control guys came. They

took Bud to the county hospital. He has mono- mon- onucleosis. And it's all Kelso's fault. He told them where I had hidden Bud. That creep,'' she cried. ''I decided to split and get a job near the hospital so I can be with Bud. But I'd like to give that creep two black eyes.'' She pulled away and looked uneasily at Chang. ''I brought you something.''

''What is it?''

''It's over there,'' she said evasively, pointing to a square object wrapped in a soiled red bandanna. ''It's. .about a person who lived at the commune for about seven months. Kelso smashed your greenhouse. And with what I brought you, Kelso should go to jail for years. Promise me, you'll put him in jail.''

''I promise.''

''Okay,'' she said tiredly.

''Help Jade to pack, Lily. Then you girls get some rest. My cousin will be here before you know it.''

When Chang picked up the phone, Lily kissed his cheek.

14

"Claire, slow down!" Luke rasped as she rounded a sharp curve and a startled fawn dashed obliquely across the road in the sweep of headlights.

"Why don't you sleep?" she replied with annoyance. But she did reduce speed. Her tone changed. She sounded on the verge of laughter. "There's where we stopped to inspect a tire. While Gil and Bob changed it, Sara and I took a walk and we found the most beautiful little brook." Abruptly she began to hum an unfamiliar tune.

Luke cringed. He rested his head against the back of the seat and half-closed his eyes. They were following the steeply ascending route of Lost Trail Pass between Idaho and Montana. Dense green walls of billowing spruce, pine and fir could not conceal the sheer granite walls and darkly plunging abysses of the Bitterroot Range. They had driven straight through from Tacoma, alternately taking the wheel and resting.

Luke knew that Claire was in another of her moods. And, of all of them—despair, indifference and abject hope—he liked her confident elation the least. She was like a person possessed. She must already feel herself cleansed of what must have been five years of guilt, sorrow and regret. Few people are given an opportunity to right an irrevocable wrong, but Claire obviously felt herself absolved. What the swing to disappointment would bring, he refused to imagine. He was certain that Christopher was not alive.

Luke's only hope of deliverance lay in turning her over to Dr. Stefan Vasa, and he tried to recall the television interview in detail. He was a short, stocky man. Hungarian. And something about a concentration camp. Himmler's insane plan to breed a blond, blue-eyed Aryan race. That was it. And, as a child, the doctor had been subjected to torture and deprivation. The scarred hands. It was coming back. The doctor's air of breeding, intelligence and erudition. Grey-black hair, the hollow dark eyes, and his repressed anger with the TV people for having tricked him into an interview. And Bob Fairway had described him as being a character out of a Gothic novel.

Dr. Stefan Vasa, Luke thought uneasily. A complex individual and certainly an unknown quantity. He decided against asking Claire for more information. She might sense what he hoped to do. Entrust her to the doctor's care.

But, as if she had perceived his trend of thought, she said softly, "It will be good to see Stefan again. I came to know him quite well the month Christopher and I stayed in Silverleaf. I learned two things about him. He loathes the Nazis and all that they represented. Unlimited evil and authority." She looked at Luke. "I suppose Bob and Sara told you. Gil and I had only been married six months when Christopher was born. Full-term. Gil was so terrified Jasper would find out, he intended to lie. Stefan told me to support Gil. He said that men who profess to know the only truth must be told lies." She looked back to the road. "The other part is his compassion for children. He was a little boy in that camp. Children were fed contaminated food, drugs that damaged their bodies and their minds. If they didn't freeze to death, they were buried in mass graves. That's why I know he would have done anything to help Christopher."

Her son, Luke thought, always her son.

The car surged forward, engine humming smoothly. Walls of granite and towering trees loomed and telescoped behind them. The searching headlights were a feeble white swath in the immense darkness. Luke studied Claire's profile. She looked lovely. Her dark hair fell around her shoulders like silk. Her expression

144

was purposeful, yet serene. For a second, she had no identity. He saw purity and strength and boundless courage, all achieved through sorrow.

Luke frowned. Nothing could have been more incongruous. He, a man wanted by the police. Claire, a grieving mother on the brink of an emotional precipice, searching for an abnormal child who might have long since died. And they were speeding through a vast wilderness to an uncertain destination, to an individual who had known the depths of human degradation and had survived.

Luke experienced a disorientation of time and place. He could sense the presence of immutable forces, so deeply imbedded in the human psyche, that the conscious mind was like a wave, crashing on a sunny sandy beach, unaware of the dark, vast currents that govern its existence.

In the next moment, the perception was lost and he was again tired, worried and uncertain of what lay ahead.

"Are you awake?" Claire asked.

"Yes."

"I think we're near the Silverleaf road. Yes. Watch for a sign on the left."

Luke spotted the sign. They were twenty miles from the village.

Claire slowed and turned to a steep, narrow gravel road. When they were a mile or so into the wild, isolated area, Claire let him drive. The road grew more rough and uneven. There wasn't a dwelling of any kind, not a light to be seen.

"Has it occurred to you," he said, "that we'll be noticed. Strangers and all that. Won't it look peculiar arriving at the motel at one in the morning?"

"When I was here before, people used to turn up at all hours. Mostly hunting and fishing parties who'd had enough of roughing it in the woods."

"How are we going to register?"

"Pick a name." She laughed softly. "The register is an old accounting journal with half the pages missing. Mr. Laroque won't recognize me. . .and don't worry. Each cabin has two bedrooms."

Luke felt again that he would like to shake her. "Just the same, you'd better keep out of his way."

Luke jerked at the steering wheel as the car skidded over a washboard section of road. Claire gasped, "Look, there's a light up ahead."

Luke slowed the car. A light, probably a lantern, was swinging in a wide, disembodied arc across the road. He punched the buttons to raise the windows and told Claire to lock her door. The car came to an idling stop.

A shabbily dressed, booted man approached the car. A rifle was cradled under his right elbow. Luke lowered the window an inch. The man peered in the back seat, then returned to Luke's window. "Where are you folks headed?"

"Silverleaf."

"Kind of late to be cruising around these parts, isn't it?"

Luke decided the best defense was an offense. "Why are you patrolling the road?"

"Not so fast. How come you're headed this way?"

Claire broke in impatiently. "We're just staying in Silverleaf for a few days."

"It's pretty cold out at night for camping."

"We're going to the motel for a quiet weekend."

The man uttered a short, humorless laugh. "Don't let it fool you. Hasn't been very quiet of late."

"Why?" Luke asked uneasily.

"It's the swamp. Trouble in the swamp. Do you know anyone up here?"

Claire nudged Luke, urging him to go on. "Yes. Dr. Stefan Vasa."

"Vasa?" A clouded look of speculation hardened the man's wrinkled face. "Well, take it easy. The

146

wildlife isn't very friendly at night." He motioned for them to go on.

Luke shoved the car into gear. The palms of his hands were damp. Fugitive fear was a way of life. The ease with which they had negotiated airports, planes, the bank where Claire had cashed a sizeable check, and the car rental agency could not eliminate that fear. "What's all this about a swamp?"

"I don't know. We loved it. It's like being on another planet. Dense foliage with white bleached tree trunks that look like ghosts. And canals everywhere. We had a picnic there, poling around in a leaky boat. That's where I fell and, as a result, Christopher was born."

Luke repressed the impossible suspicion that the trouble in the swamp would be Christopher. It had to be the wildlife.

A few darkened shacks began to dot either side of the road.

"Keep going," Claire urged. "The motel is on the other side of the village."

The other side turned out to be less than a half mile away. The main street was dark and deserted. The false-fronted, wooden buildings advertised their services. Pop's General Store, Marie's Cafe, Waren G. Watts, Hardware. Bow's Museum. The long porch of a dimly lit saloon on a corner was occupied by two armed men.

"It looks like a town in a TV western," Luke said.

"That's what we thought." She pointed out Dr. Vasa's clinic, a small, white modern structure which stood out conspicuously. But the motel looked less than comfortable. And it seemed deserted, too. Claire started to get out of the car.

"You'd better stay out of sight. I'll go." Luke punched a bell to the left of the door. It was some time before a heavy-set man, running to fat, with trousers and a sweater pulled over pajamas, appeared. "Mr.

147

Laroque?''

''Name's Al,'' He yawned.

''We'd like a cabin for a couple of days.''

Laroque peered at Claire in the car, turned and trudged into the office. He returned with a dangling key. ''Number six, at the end. That'll be twenty dollars in advance.''

Luke dug for his wallet. He decided to risk a question. ''Is anyone else staying here?''

''No. That's funny.'' He scratched his head. ''A couple of strangers, passing through, having a drink in the saloon, asked me the same thing. . .you can sign the book in the morning.'' He slammed the door.

Shortly, Claire and Luke were safely locked in. The cabin was surprisingly pleasant. A closet of a kitchen and a small bathroom divided the two bedrooms. A pot-bellied stove dominated the main room.

''What's wrong?'' she asked. Luke was drawing flowered curtains, testing the locks on the windows.

''Nothing.''

''Should we have a fire? It's cold.''

''No, let's wait until morning.''

She nodded and disappeared into one of the bedrooms. Luke fell into bed, but not to sleep. The sounds of the forest were unfamiliar and disturbing. And once shots rang out and a car—it sounded like a jeep—raced to the east.

Luke pounded his pillow. When he had telephoned Belden Beach from Tacoma, he had told Chang about the brown van near Claire's apartment. Chang's anxiety had erupted. ''You're probably safe enough from arrest. But, my God, any place that size is a trap! Stay in the village but stay out of sight.''

So, now, the unanswerable question was—who were the two inquisitive strangers?

Luke resolutely closed his eyes. He hadn't told Claire, and he tried not to think about it himself.

15

In the morning, around six, Chang would have more than welcomed an invigorating swim, but, on the off-chance that Luke might call again, he took a long hot and cold shower to relieve his cramped muscles and the bruise on the back of his head. He had slept in a chair, waiting for his cousin's call to say that they had arrived safely in Los Angeles.

While he prepared and ate his breakfast, he scanned the morning paper. There was little that was new. The Survival Kit hearings were still scheduled to open the next Monday. Suppositions and intimations of menace still lingered about Christopher Dorn. And the LAPD anticipated an arrest very soon. Did that mean that the police knew where Claire and Luke had gone?

Digby's column in the *Times* contained a new development. "It seems that Jasper Dorn was human, after all. In a brief statement by Judge Josephine B. Davis, Dorn named as one of his heirs, Marcella Eilers, 78 years old and a black, who for some years worked for Dorn. But in what capacity, it is not known. Obviously, theirs was not a romantic relationship, but the secrecy surrounding her services leads to the speculation that she might have assisted Dorn in another of his secretive schemes. Matthew Powell could not be reached for comment. This reporter does not believe that Dorn's attitude toward his deformed grandson and his son's bereaved widow was one of concern and generosity. Quite to the contrary, his obsession with his impeccable public image most certainly dictated concealment of the existence of a grossly ill member of his family. Until all the heirs of Dorn's estate have reported to the court, the truth will not be revealed but I predict that full disclosure will be a blockbuster."

Chang thrust the papers aside. So, now, another facet of Dorn's secretive life was about to emerge, Chang thought. Another strange growth had blossomed on the malignant plant.

He glanced at the phone. He was tempted to call Luke in Silverleaf at Laroque's Motel, the only one in the village, according to the Missoula Chamber of Commerce. But he decided against it. He could not be sure of the names Claire and Luke were using.

The house, without Jade, seemed intensely lonely and he finally went out to the greenhouse, salvaging some of the plants, collecting mounds of broken glass, smashed flower pots and scattered earth. Frequently, he took out Laotse's *Book of Tao*, concentrating on its well-remembered lines. Until he could achieve some measure of serenity and objectivity, a way to restore it to its vital role in his life would continue to elude him. Was he to look forward to a decade or two of retirement with this feeling of isolation and worthlessness?

Just before nine, he called Barker at the substation, telling him about the greenhouse. "I want Kelso arrested. Charge him with wilful destruction of personal property."

Barker said that he would send someone out to the commune that afternoon. He was moderately sympathetic about Chang's loss, but he was so full of recent developments that they burst out in a flood.

"Fremont and Claire Dorn have been located!"

Chang's spirits hit bottom.

Barker went on to explain. Apparently, a routine check on all flights to Canada, Mexico and South America hadn't paid off. But a counter agent at Western Airlines remembered a young woman, answering Claire Dorn's description, accompanied by a tall, thin bearded guy, who could have been Fremont. They flew to Tacoma. She rented a car in the name of Jean

150

Mason. Identification, driver's license, credit cards, the works. Matthew Powell found a Jean Mason in Dorn's private address book so it had to be the Dorn daughter-in-law. "Powell thinks they're headed for Silverleaf, Montana, where the Dorn grandson was born. It's only about five hundred miles from Tacoma. Friday morning when the courts open, extradition papers on Fremont will be issued and Mintner is flying up there to arrest him. Say, isn't the latest Dorn heir something? A 78-year-old black woman? That Dorn had more going for him than a one-armed juggler. Chang, are you there? Chang?"

Chang had hung up.

Claire and Luke were in deadly peril. Not only from false arrest. But much worse. If Powell hadn't known where they were going, he certainly knew now.

Chang settled down at the telephone, calling airlines to find the most expeditious way of flying to Silverleaf and finally made reservations for an early afternoon flight to Missoula where he would rent a car. He hurriedly packed a small suitcase. When he went to the telephone table to get his revolver, he saw Lily's kerchief-wrapped package. He thrust it in his bag.

At noon he took a local taxi to Los Angeles International Airport.

16

Dr. Stefan Vasa crossed the diffusely-lit, austere living room to the elaborate stereo on an inner wall. The final notes of Bartok's *Dance Suite* faded. He switched off the hi-fi and stood for a moment, wide shoulders drawn forward, hands resting on the cabinet.

Pushing at her dark hair, Claire flashed a troubled look at Luke who nodded an encouragement he did not feel. Dr. Vasa had been unable to see them during the long, uneasy day—a medical emergency—but he had invited them to dine at his lodge. From the moment of their arrival the atmosphere had been inhospitable. It was partly due to the presence of the sullen, unfriendly woman, Al Laroque's wife, who had cooked and served the dinner. And the doctor had pointedly avoided discussion about Claire's son and their fugitive status. He had dominated the conversation at the table with anecdotes of his own traumatic childhood and his present life in the village.

Luke's conception of his personality and character had considerably altered. Instead of the compassion and hatred for authority, that Claire had described, Vasa seemed to be supremely indifferent, living in a self-contained world of intellectual pleasures and, for contrast, an undemanding work. But his complex mind revealed subleties, far beyong average comprehension. And his comments and observations indicated that his reactions could not be foreseen.

Now, without turning, Vasa said in his faintly accented voice, "It's such an extraordinary question, Claire, I feel it requires explanation. Your son is what? More than five years old. And yet you think he might have come here?"

He turned. "But let us enjoy more wine." He filled

their crystal goblets from the slender green bottle. His hands, except for the webbing of scars, were finely proportioned with a slender grace. Holding his glass by its stem, he raised it, examining the pale amber liquid appreciatively.

"One can only savor life fully by experiencing its opposites. For example, this wine, whose secret belongs to an ancient vinery on the Rhine, and the melody we just heard, first perceived by the soul of a poet and translated into musical language, as opposed to the proximity of our primitive heritage." He inclined his head toward the wide windows beneath which a vast expanse of heavily wooded forest could be indistinctly seen. And felt. A rising wind gave the trees and rocky terrain a vicarious life. "Out there," Vasa murmured, "is the ultimate source of myth and of man. It is an experience to be shared, is it not, Mr. Fremont?"

What a time to philosophize, Luke thought impatiently. He had decided that the most persuasive way to impress the doctor with Claire's unstable condition was to let her tell the tragic story of her son's brief years. In itself, the tale was bizarre. But imbued with emotional excesses, Vasa couldn't help but recognize her emotional problems. Now, Luke wasn't certain of what Vasa's reaction might be.

In fact, the entire day had been unsettling and strange, a day of unresolved perceptions. Far from being the idyllic refuge Vasa had extolled during dinner, the village and its people were unfriendly, suspicious. And there was fear, too. When Claire and Luke had ventured out cautiously for lunch, conversations among the villagers fragmented in their presence and seemed to center on the swamp and a silent resentment of Vasa. Yet the doctor seemed serenely unaware of the turmoil.

And then there was Claire. Luke looked at her now as she raised her glass. During the long afternoon, cooped up in the motel which he had anticipated with reluctance, she had been a stimulating companion, speaking of music and books, impersonal yet essential facets of life. She even understood much of what went on at Enterprises. She did not mention her son, nor did she refer to the climactic moment, Vasa's answer to her question, which would end, Luke was certain, in despair. But she could endure. This quality must have sustained her in her relationship with her father-in-law. Luke had wondered what marriage to a girl like Claire might have been. Unlike Lori and her pursuit of mindless pleasure, Claire was capable of love, strength and a shared purpose. But there his fantasy had dissolved. Claire's unswerving dedication to her doomed son had distorted her life. Her strength was drawn from that single source.

Vasa asked Luke again if a greater understanding of one's values was to be found in the proximity of such opposites.

Luke said bluntly, "Doctor, I hope you understand why Claire came to see you. And how perilous my own position is."

Vasa dismissed Luke's comment with a shrug of his wide shoulders. "Your problems are your own, Mr. Fremont. I can assure you that I, in no way, will add to them." He sat near Claire on the couch. "Now, my dear, suppose you tell me why you think your son, who is little more than an infant, might be here?"

"He wouldn't look five years old, Stefan. He might appear to be fully grown. I don't know. I don't know what he looks like. Surely you've seen the newspapers and the sketches?"

"Yes. But I should like to hear your version of what has happened."

Claire cast another uncertain look at Luke, then described the first early months of her son's abnormally rapid physical and mental development; his ability to think, to understand, although he couldn't speak. Luke couldn't restrain a feeling of admiration. However illogical her hopes were, she spoke with conviction and objectivity.

"After Gil died, I had to tell his father everything. Jasper didn't seem shocked; he insisted on the best of treatment and care. But after Christopher was sent to the nursing home, I was not permitted to see him and I was not told anything about his tests and treatment. I have since learned, he responded to none of it. He continued to grow alarmingly, particularly his head and his hands and feet. There were psychological problems, violent rages." She faltered. "Christopher escaped, killed an orderly and disappeared. He was seen running on a freeway. That was about a year ago. In an atlas I had sent him, I discovered maps of the Western states had been torn out. He must have intended coming here. Where he was born." Claire became very pale, lips moving soundlessly. Then she said, "Stefan, have you seen him? Is he here?"

Vasa took her hands and, for the first time, extended sympathy. "My dear, Silverleaf is a very small village. Anyone with such an extraordinary appearance would have been noticed instantly. I know your disappointment will be acute. But, no, your son is not here."

Luke frowned. Vasa had not answered Claire's question specifically. He had answered for the villagers, but not for himself.

Claire gave a small cry and fell back against the couch, closing her eyes.

Vasa touched her forehead. "She has a slight fever. Has she been ill?"

"She had some sort of a virus two days ago."

"She should not have have undertaken the trip here."

"No one could have prevented it."

"I'm all right," she said indistinctly. She attempted to sit up.

"You'd better take her back to the motel," Vasa said. "I'll give you some medication—"

"I think she'd be better off in the clinic."

"I have no qualified RN on duty at night."

"Stefan," Claire murmurmed, "couldn't I lie down for a time. I feel so ill. So tired."

She did look on the verge of collapse, Luke thought worriedly "What she needs," Luke said, hoping it was true, "is a good night's sleep."

Claire slipped to the cushions on the couch and lay there inertly. "Sleep," she murmured. "Stay here."

"Here!" Vasa said sharply. He appeared to be thinking it over. "Yes. An antibiotic to clear up any lingering infection. And a sedative. With adequate rest, she should feel quite recovered tomorrow. I'll see to the room." He left quickly.

Luke sat beside her.

"I'm sorry," she said with difficulty. "I think I knew all along it was hopeless."

"Don't talk, Claire."

"Thank you," she whispered. "Thank you, boy scout."

When Dr. Vasa returned, Luke lifted her in his arms. He was astonished at how little she weighed. She stiffened, then relaxed. Her head fell against his shoulder. There was complete trust in the way she lay against him. When he placed her on the turned-down bed, Vasa found that there was no water in the carafe on the nightstand and left the room. Claire's eyes flashed open.

"You must rest," Luke said, beginning to feel that being a boy scout had its advantages. He was also astonished at his reaction. The perfect opportunity to release Claire to the doctor's care had presented itself, and he found he was reluctant to do so.

156

"Luke," she whispered urgently. "There's something wrong. Stefan is. . .I'm not all that sick. . .I'll stay here and try to find out. . .you watch what he does from the outside—"

Vasa had returned, holding out a glass and two capsules.

Luke was mystified. What had she noticed?

Vasa was drawing curtains and switching off lights. Luke had another glimpse of the plea in Claire's eyes before the room became dark.

In the large main room Luke asked for a brandy. A drink would give him an opportunity to stay a moment longer.

Vasa splashed cognac into a single snifter and handed it to Luke. "I rarely indulge after dinner."

"Claire hoped desperately her son might be here," he began tentatively.

"I know." Vasa shook his head. "That young woman has had too much tragedy in her life. This experience only added to it. Why did you come with her?"

"Silverleaf seemed a safe place."

"If you are recognized, I shall be forced to reveal that I have seen you. You had better leave, as soon as possible. Tomorrow, if Claire has recovered."

Luke had downed the brandy and asked the only direct question he could think of. "What's going on in the swamp? Could the boy be hiding there?"

Luke was rewarded by a faint flicker of anxiety on Vasa's impassive face. "So you've seen all the ignorant posturing. You've heard the foolish suspicions of the villagers?"

"Yes." Luke related briefly what he had observed. Willie Bow, the man patrolling the Silverleaf road, men gathering in small hostile groups on the street, women restraining their children from straying too far. "The villagers are frightened."

157

Vasa looked through the windows to the dark wilderness. "You must comprehend their mentality. They could be living in the last century. They're guided by ignorance and superstition, all derived from their primitive relationship with nature. I have tried to impart a scientifically informed knowledge to them but they refuse to acknowledge it."

Luke was puzzled. A man with as much sophisticated perception as Vasa possessed should have been more sensitive to the unfriendly atmosphere. Particularly since some of it was directed at him. "Their fear is real enough," Luke insisted. "And it's connected with the swamp."

"The swamp is a wildlife refuge and is overpopulated. I sent several requests to the Fish and Wildlife Service of the Department of Interior to re-open the area to hunting and fishing. Nothing has been done. Another example of the lethargy of official action. Last winter was exceptionally frigid. Animals were forced to forage for food."

The doctor slid smoothly into his explanation. In foraging for food, the animals had discovered cultivated crops and storage silos and sheds, a much more accessible source of sustenance. Naturally a number of unfortunate incidents were destined to occur. A toddler was attacked by a large waterrat in a mobile camper. An amateur photographer had an unpleasant encounter with a flock of large birds. "This morning I had to treat wounds inflicted on a farmer whose gardens were invaded by a group of wild pigs. As a matter of fact, I promised to look in on him tonight. I must go to the clinic."

Luke, hoping to prolong their conversation, offered to drive the doctor down.

"No, I'll take my own car. You return tomorrow around noon. If Claire is well enough, I strongly advise you to leave."

Luke found himself alone on the flagged stone terrace. He kicked at the fluttering brown leaves as he walked toward his car.

His feeling of responsibility toward Claire had grown. Her suspicions about the doctor could well be another facet of her instability, but her courage and determination in staying at the lodge were undeniable. And everything the doctor had said about the villagers was logical enough. But Vasa's denial of Christopher's presence had been evasive.

After driving a half mile on the narrow dirt road, Luke parked the car in the deep shadows of a group of pine trees and dense undergrowth. When he switched off the engine, the sighing wind emphasized the endless wilderness. Five minutes passed and he heard no sound of an engine. Nor did the lights of the doctor's car pass him on the road.

Luke thought of Claire, asleep and defenseless in the lodge. Not even trying to rationalize his behavior, he trudged back up the curving dirt road as quietly as he could. Within viewing distance of the doctor's lodge, he sat down in the deep shadow of a clump of trees to wait, trying not to think about Chang's anxious advice about staying in the village.

17

With unswerving attention, Chang had driven the steeply ascending route of Lost Trail Pass. A light rain, more like fog, was falling, and the sheer granite walls, thickly massed trees and precipices were only a misted blur. The windshield wipers of the rented maroon sedan thrummed erratically. He had almost missed the turn-off to Silverleaf and now, with no white guide line on the rough road, he had the eerie sensation that the car was inching forward in a watery black desolate void. When the driver of an oncoming car dimmed his headlights twice, as the cars bumped passed each other, Chang responded, grateful for the friendly gesture. The grey car disappeared, and he was immersed in the black void again.

While airborne and in the car, he had attempted to find the answer to a single question—What did Luke Fremont know that posed such a threat to Matthew Powell?

Chang's knowledge of Luke's personal life was meager, but he reviewed what little he did know in the event some point had been overlooked. Luke had been raised in an orphanage. . .a fine education due to scholarships. . .an interview before graduation from Michigan State had resulted in his job with Dorn Enterprises. Luke had said, "No big deal. I was one of a half dozen guys." The unfortunate marriage to Foxy Doxy Lady who had admired powerful men like Dorn. Was there a connection? Chang doubted it. She was in Greece and out of Luke's life. Besides, Dorn's machinations had been political, not extramarital. Chang's last bit of information was as useless. Luke often recalled the name Percy. It was the name he had used when he had gone to the disco. But, as Luke had said, Percy was probably one of the kids at the orphanage.

Chang sighed gustily. He concentrated on another bumpy, watery mile and then re-phrased his question—What did Matthew Powell know that was threatened by Luke's very existence?

There was no answer to that, either.

Chang checked the odometer. He was still some eight or nine miles from the village. He saw a faint flash of headlights behind him in the rearview mirror, growing rapidly brighter. The approaching car was moving much faster than he felt was prudent and, as the car neared, Chang pulled to the right so it could pass. The automobile. . .grey, like the first car he had seen?. . .pulled abreast to the left of him and stayed there. Uneasily, Chang peered through the mist-drenched windows. He saw two men, formless in heavy coats, sitting in the front seat.

Why didn't they move on?

And then Chang leaned forward tensely, clutching the wheel. The grey car was forcing him nearer the shallow ditch on his side of the road. He tapped his horn. No response. He slowed; the other did, also. And then he realized what was intended.

Just ahead, a narrow wooden bridge spanned what appeared to be a narrow deep gully. And with the cars positioned as they were, he could be easily forced against the rail and over the side.

Chang jammed his foot on the accelerator.

He shot ahead and reached the bridge first. Wooden planks creaked and reverberated as his car gained momentum. Halfway across, there was a sharp impact, and the rear of his car slewed toward the rail. Chang swerved left and heard the wrenching tear of metal as fenders crumpled. He was still inches in the lead and, reaching the far side of the bridge, floored the accelerator, willing the car forward against the backward pull of gravity. The car shuddered, water spraying on both sides, mud and gravel splattering all the windows. He began to swerve from side to side, blocking his pursuers. The silent race with disaster seemed endless, although it was a matter of minutes before both cars skidded around a sharp curve. Chang saw a feeble arc of light, swinging in the middle of the road.

He leaned on the horn.

Seconds later, there was a vicious jolt, and Chang's car flew into the ditch, nose buried in underbrush. The motor stalled. Dazedly, he slumped against the wheel, horn still blasting, as he struggled to breath. Vaguely, he heard someone shouting and managed to open his door.

"God Almighty! What happened?"

Chang saw a thin man, dressed in heavy clothes, a dripping hat pulled low over his forehead. There was a rifle under an arm.

"What happened?"

"I'm not sure," Chang said, still gulping for air.

"Looks like they were trying to shove you off the road. Them drunk hunters. Passed through yesterday. Are you hurt?"

"Not much." Chang had discovered a gash on his left knee. "Where did they go?"

"When they saw my light, they shoved you in the ditch, backed and took off down the road. It sure looks like your bus is parked for the night."

Chang stared. The uplifted back wheels were still spinning in air. "I guess it will have to be towed out."

"Yeah, the garage. Ask for Ed."

Chang leaned weakly against the crumpled fender, aware that, in the light of the lantern, his Oriental features were being noticed for the first time. "Where are you headed?" his saviour asked suspiciously.

"The village, now." Chang took his dufflebag from the car.

"Yeah, well, my name's Bow, Willie Bow. You look pretty green. I've got a thermos of coffee back in my jeep. Come on."

As the men trudged up the road, Chang half-listened to another and more detailed description of his accident, while the implications of the nightmare episode thudded into focus like bricks on a wall.

He must have been followed from L.A. International to Missoula where he had rented the car. The two men in the grey automobile were already in Silverleaf and had been contacted. These two must have trailed Claire and Luke. And they had carefully inspected the road for a spot where an accident was likely to occur and had selected the bridge.

Chang sipped the coffee with a shaking hand. Matthew Powell's strategy was more devious and encompassing that it had seemed at first. And it had grown to include Chang. Again, the unanswerable question, why?

Chang found he was too spent to speculate. But, of one thing, he was certain. Luke and Claire must leave Silverleaf with him, immediately.

A cup of coffee later, Willie Bow gave Chang a lift into the village and shot back to his road patrol.

Chang limped the length of the main street. The false-fronted stores were dark and deserted, but a spill of yellow light from the swinging doors of the saloon slashed a narrow path across the street. He could hear a subdued swell of voices. There were a number of shotguns propped against the railing on the porch.

Chang was reminded, not of a TV western, but of a frontier town where lethal action preempted explanation.

The Silverleaf motel was just ahead. Only one of the cabins was illuminated and that very faintly. It must be the one where Luke and Claire were staying. There were sounds of departure from the saloon and

Chang moved silently to the empty carport. The door was locked but under pressure the lock snapped. He called out cautiously. There was no answer.

To his dismay, the cabin was deserted.

After bathing his injured knee and changing into dry clothing, Chang found it was too cold to relax and reached for his bag and an extra sweater. His fingers touched Lily's kerchief-wrapped package. At last, in total privacy, he took it out and untied the knots. It was a dog-earred copybook. A piece of paper was clipped to the cover.

"Chang, he lived mostly in chains in that hut at the commune for about six months. I loved him. When he wanted to leave, I helped him to escape. I hope this will show how that creep Kelso treated him. Like an animal. I hope this will put Kelso in jail. Lily."

Chang turned to the first page. The block-printed letters were uneven and laboriously erased or scratched over. He read, "MY NAME IS CHRISTOPHER DORN."

18

Something rustled in the bushes behind him, and Luke spun around, peering in the black shadowed foliage. He had waited so long in the enveloping darkness of the slight rise to one side of Dr. Vasa's lodge that he had begun to fear the real reason for the doctor's abrupt dismissal was not the need to check on a patient, but only an excuse to speed an unwelcome guest. Namely, himself.

The rise gave him a distant view of the road, winding up to the front of the lodge, and a closer watch on the back entrance. Bow's warning that there were dangerous animals roaming the area at night made Luke long for the safety of the motel cabin. Safety in the cabin? There might be human predators waiting for him there.

Again, he wondered what had made Claire suspicious of the doctor. There had been no lights in what he assumed was her room. But the thought of her there with Vasa in the lodge was intensely unsettling.

Luke rubbed his hands, breathing heavily on them. The temperature had begun to drop; a fine misty rain had just begun to fall. He leaned forward tensely.

A faint swath of light briefly illuminated the back entrance. Vasa, carrying a package and wearing a dark sweater and trousers, took off up the road behind the lodge. He disappeared rapidly but he had snapped on a flashlight. Luke stumbled to his feet, feeling stiff and cold, and followed as closely as he could.

It was a nightmare of a blind hike. After a few hundred yards, the road dwindled to a path, then to some unmarked, ascending route, which Vasa followed without hesitation but with practiced ease. He must have done it many times. The trees became sparse, and they began to descend sharply over sliding wet shale and around convoluted ridges of granite. More than once Luke feared he had lost the flicker of the flash, only to round a protruding crag to see its glow just ahead.

Abruptly the light disappeared as if it had been snuffed out like a candle. Luke felt his way along a narrow ledge, pebbles dropping into a black void where he heard them plunge into an unseen pool of water. He sank to his knees and crept forward, slipping on the wet rock. The sounds of dripping water were quite loud as he reached an angled V of rock, a cul de sac. Groping hazardously, he blindly searched for the angular descent Vasa must have followed, but he couldn't find it.

The sounds of dripping water grew louder. He must be somewhere near the swamp. Breathing hard, he crouched. After a rest, he would back his way from the ledge and climb to higher ground. But how he would find his way to the village, he didn't know. Probably the best plan would be to find some comparatively safe spot, and hopefully dry, and wait until daylight. He hoped Vasa wouldn't emerge as suddenly as he had vanished.

A piercing, echoing whistle made his heart pound. And then he heard Vasa's accented voice, "Are you here? Answer me. Where are you?" He whistled again.

There was no way to determine where the whistle was coming from. But a break, somewhere in the convoluted crevices, was carrying the sound.

Vasa called again and again and finally there was an answering voice, at first, faintly heard then more clearly. Voice? It was a hollow, gutteral, elongated moaning, as if the sounds issued from a constricted throat where the tongue was an impediment, not an aid to speech. The words were unintelligible although they had the cadence of speech.

"It's about time," Vasa said in discernible relief. "Where have you been?"

There was another spate of moaning explanation which, apparently Vasa could understand.

"You were following two men on the road, again? I told you to stay away from the village. And now it is imperative that you do so."

Silence.

"Do you understand me, Christopher?"

Christopher!

Luke grabbed at an arm of rock to avoid falling. In his desire to listen, he had moved dangerously near the crumbling rim of the ledge. Dislodged pebbles trickled in a noisy stream, splashing into the void of water. Vasa must have heard it for he was silent for a moment.

Christopher! Claire had been right all along. Her son was in Silverleaf. And Vasa had concealed it for some reason.

The hollow, laborious groan continued as if protesting Vasa's peremptory manner.

"We've been over this a number of times." the doctor seemed to be pleading. "How many times have I explained it to you? You're comfortable here and safe. You know the people in the village wouldn't accept you as one of them."

Luke felt a deeper cold penetrate his body. It was fear. What must Christopher be? What must he look like?

Now Vasa sounded angry. "New people have come here. There is much danger. To save yourself, you must stay here, out of sight. Everything is arranged. Passports, identification papers. And money. All are in my safe in the study. I've shown them to you."

The unintelligible groan became a rising snarl, angry and defiant.

"I know our departure has been postponed. But this time it is certain, as soon as we can leave without

167

being seen. Once we are safely away, you'll be free. Isn't that what you've always wanted? To be free of restraint? Free of hatred and suspicion? To live the way you want to?''

The snarling took on a mournful tone, like the pathetic cry of a tortured animal.

''You have suffered, but it's almost over. Think who and what you are, Christopher. The powers you possess. Remember our plans for the future.''

The ensuing moan must have been some sort of agreement for Vasa sounded satisfied that his instructions were going to be obeyed. ''Very good. There will be no more meetings at my lodge at night. And you must stay in the swamp. When I next come, in a day or two, it will be time for us to leave. Here. I brought you bread and cheese. I know you don't like it. But it's the kind of food you must eat until we arrive at our destination. And, here. A shirt and trousers. You must wear them when we leave. Now, I must get back to the lodge.''

Luke didn't wait for the end of the conversation. As quickly and as quietly as he could, he inched his way backward to a wider space where he could turn and climb out of the crevice, tearing at spiky bushes and small trees, anything that would facilitate finding some place of concealment. He found a depression above the ledge none too soon. Vasa was breathing heavily as he passed. And guided by the pinpoint of light, Luke followed the doctor through the dark wilderness.

The eastern sky was faintly streaked with dawn by the time the unaware guide and the weary guided reached the lodge. Vasa slipped inside. Luke resisted the impulse to burst in and forcibly remove Claire. He was wild with fear and uncertainty.

When the lodge was dark, Luke trudged down the winding road to where the rented car was concealed.

Obviously, Vasa was planning to move Christopher somewhere. From all indications, the plan was complicated and purposeful. Claire must be told as much as she could rationally handle. But what should be done after that, Luke could not imagine. Force Vasa to talk? Try to seek out Christopher and persuade him to accept a change of plans? The horror of the sketches seemed to be cemented in Luke's mind. What manner of approach? What means of communication? An unknown entity, who did not wear clothes, who did not eat normal food and who lived in a swamp?

Luke had reached the motel and drove into the carport. The unlocked door made his pulses pound. Entering warily, he whirled about at a sound from his bedroom.

"Luke?"

"My God! Chang!"

The men stared at each other in silence.

Finally Luke said, "Christopher is alive. He's here."

"I know," Chang said and held up the copybook.

19

"My name is Christopher Dorn. Lily is my friend in the commune. She couldn't teach me to talk. She taught me to read and print. This is my story. I am over four years old, but I am taller than Lily. From the time I was born in Silverleaf, Montana, I understood what people said. I didn't know this was different. I said all the words I heard, but they didn't come out right. No one could understand me. So I watched another baby in the clinic and I saw that new babies shouldn't talk or jump or run. So I did these things when I was alone. Except for my mother Claire. She didn't understand but it didn't make her angry. When I was a month old in Palos Verdes, I knew my father Gilbert hated me. He said I was a bastard *freak*. When I was five months old, he wanted to kill me. But he fell off the balcony. I felt that I would be free to run and jump. And not lie in a bed. That was when I learned that whatever I am, it is wrong. I was moved to a nursing home and it was the beginning of hate for me. My grandfather Jasper and my mother Claire never came to see me. The doctors were afraid of me. I was tied to beds and chairs. The orderly Groder hated me and called me a freak. He liked to do things, when I was tied, to hurt me.

"*Freak*. For a long time I did not know what it meant. Some kind of bird or animal?

"I killed the orderly Groder to get his clothes. People wear them. Lily says I should not tell this, but why should I lie? When I escaped from the nursing home, I took the maps which showed me how to go to Silverleaf. I ran for a long time. The road was a freeway which I liked. Free. Lily was driving a car and asked me to ride with her. In the car mirror I saw my face for the first time. My head was too big. Why? Lily's husband Bud and a man who is sick'in the head, named Kelso both looked at my big head and hands and feet and called me a *freak*. Lily was nice to me so I stayed in the commune. I worked, doing heavy, hard things they could not do. I was very good stealing because I could climb and run and jump very fast. One time a lot of people came to the commune, and Kelso made me do all my tricks, he called them. Climbing a greasy pole, running fast, jumping, lifting people and cars, drinking and eating things that made other people sick. I can sleep, wake up, stop my heart beating when I want to. And Kelso scratched my back with a knife. The long cut was bleeding and I made it go away. It is easy to do. Someone said, he is a freak. We could have a traveling show called The Freak. We had a fight but I couldn't keep so many away from me, and Kelso chained and locked me in a little house where I couldn't move again.

"Why do people want me not to move? My body needs to move, and when I can't it makes me angry. In the dark, chained to the floor, I knew I must go to Silverleaf to see Dr. Vasa. My mother liked him, and I hope he can explain why I am different. He will explain why people hate and are afraid of me.

"I watched television for four years, but I still do not understand. Why do people wear shoes and clothes? I have skin on my feet that keeps them from hurting. Why do people laugh and cry? Emotions have nothing to do with living. Why do they eat cooked food? Why are they all weak and not strong? Why do they feel heat and cold? Why do they ride in cars and planes when it is so much easier to run? Why do they fight each other with guns and bombs? Why did all the doctors say I was sick in my body and in my head when I know I am stronger than anyone? Why do people do things that keep them from living? I hope

Dr. Vasa can answer these questions. If he does, then I will know why I am a freak.

"Living is the most important thing of all. Anything or anyone who tries to take my living from me, will not live himself. I must run and hunt and sleep. I must be free. Lily is going to help me to escape. I will run at night and hide during the day so people cannot see me. I will hide in country barns or old houses. Animals do not hate or fear me. And they eat good food.

"Why do people not know that sunrise and sunset are the rules of living?

"Lily will keep my story. I cannot take it with me. I hope Dr. Vasa will send for it. (Signed) CHRISTOPHER DORN."

Luke dropped the copybook and stared at Chang in stunned amazement. "This is incredible! My God! What kind of a creature is he?"

Chang shook his head. "I don't know. Perhaps it's the result of a genetic defect. Or an injury before birth."

"Claire's fall in the swamp?"

"It's possible, I suppose."

"But the cruelty! Confined in a cell for years. Chained in a hut. And all those tests and treatment. Why couldn't the doctors find out about him?"

"He didn't trust anyone. Why should he have? Except for Lily who apparently accepted him as a normal person. And, obviously, medicine has no test or treatment for this deviation from what is called normal."

"What could Vasa be planning to do with him? They're going away someplace." Luke related the information about identification papers and how Vasa had ordered Christopher to stay in the swamp until it was safe to leave.

"The boy also came to trust Vasa. Perhaps the doctor has learned the causes of his condition. And I suspect the villagers have spotted him. They know the boy is in the swamp. That's the reason for the road patrol, the shotguns everywhere.''

Luke jumped to his feet. "Claire! She's up at Vasa's lodge. She suspected something was wrong last night and pretended she was ill. God, Chang, I've got to get her out of there. The boy thinks she deserted him. She could be in danger.''

"And so are you." As briefly as possible. Chang told Luke about Captain Leo Stone's minor role in Dorn's death which now seemed to be part of Matthew Powell's elaborate plot against Luke. "His men are here. Two of them. This time they won't fail. We must leave the motel, make it look as if you have left Silverleaf. After you collect Claire, we must leave the village. Sheriff Mintner is arriving sometime during the weekend with extradition papers to take you back to Los Angeles.''

"I'm picking Claire up today at noon.''

Chang glanced at the curtained window. The bright rectangle dimmed the single lighted bulb in the cabin. He switched it off. "Then we've got to go someplace where we won't be seen. Hide your car. What about the swamp?''

"The boy is there!''

"That's a chance we'll have to take. I doubt that anyone would go there alone. He'd want the village with him. You go on foot to the lodge. I'll go back to the village, retrieve my car and pick up you and Claire. Then we'll decide where to go. Just remember, stay away from the village.''

Luke picked up the copybook. "What about this? Should Claire read it?''

"Don't you think she should? She'll learn it sooner or later. But the doctor must not see it. It might panic him into leaving immediately. Vasa won't find it easy to leave, though. The villagers will see to that.''

Chang's prediction was more accurate than he ever could have imagined.

173

20

The bi-weekly public bus which delivered mail, pack-ages, supplies and summer vacationers to Silverleaf, which was its last stop before it retraced its circuitous route through the sheer mountain pass, was nearing the Silverleaf plateau. The driver, a scrawny, middle-aged man yawned, anticipating the breakfast he would enjoy at Marie's Cafe.

As the bus labored up a last series of hair-pin curves, an overturned maroon sedan blocked a portion of the road. Windows were smashed, glass littered the tarmac and doors were ajar. The driver whistled. It wasn't the first pile-up he had come across, and it wouldn't be the last. There was scarcely enough room for him to angle around the wreck where he pulled to the side of the road and swung down. He would have to inform the Forestry Station in the mountains, north of the village, as the rangers were the only official authority in the area. The driver grinned. All those fellows did all day was sit on their butts, looking for smoke signals.

The driver circled the car, but saw no one pinned underneath it or lying on the road. Frowning, he noticed a wide swath of oil-splattered gravel from the ditch to the present position of the car. It seemed like the car had been pulled out of the ditch. There was a break in the dense fall undergrowth beyond the ditch. It looked like someone had left the scene. The driver was not about to explore. He would leave that to the authorities.

Then he spotted a rifle in the shadowed undergrowth and peered cautiously. He saw a booted leg, twisted at a peculiar angle. He pushed on a few steps and let out a hoarse shout.

"Jesus!"

The dead man was Willie Bow, his arms and legs flung like those of a rag doll. His bulging eyes were frozen in a gaping stare.

The driver backed off hastily and ran heavily toward the bus. He jammed it into motion. He had always thought the village talk about a monstrosity living in the swamp was a bunch of hogwash. But it must be true. Willie Bow's bones had been snapped like a handful of matches.

The old bus careened around the last curve into the village. This would put the cap on the trouble that had been brewing since spring. He decided to tell Al Laroque first. He would know what to do.

21

The entrance to the swamp was a narrow, marshy passage between sheer, rocky walls. Near the entrance a few leaky dories were tied to a water-bleached rotting jetty. At first, the swamp looked impenetrable, a forest of dense, sun-flecked foliage and whitened rotted trunks of trees, convoluted ridges of glaciated granite, dotted with caves, tufted islands of mossy weeds, separated by winding channels of muddy water and narrow trails. The green-shadowed light, after the brilliant early morning sun outside, was dim, indistinct. It might have been evening.

It was so quiet. A threatening silence, because the sounds of ordinary life—traffic, radios, footsteps, a dog barking—were absent. Gradually Chang realized that it was not silence, but sounds which were rarely heard, which existed centuries before man-made noise was recorded on the ancient sound track of time. Dripping water, a snapping twig, the slithery plot and splash of an unseen creature, diving for its prey in the murky channels. A sudden raucous shriek, signifying death and the victor's triumph in the endless struggle for existence.

Chang had selected the dory that looked the least waterlogged and, having boarded it carefully, was sitting in the bow. Luke had left for Vasa's lodge an hour ago, and Chang had been trying to correlate the existence of an abnormal child—or was Christopher supranormal?—with the insidious pattern of events, Dorn's death and Powell's venomous plot against Luke. Any logical connection continued to elude him. He had tried to envision the child himself. Christopher was a composite of disparate impressions: a deformed creation of medical fact and artistic imagination; a human entity who could be loved as shown by Lily's note; a homo sapiens capable of logical thought, however subhuman his set of values; and finally, from Luke's description of the unseen encounter with Vasa in the swamp, a mute creature, capable only of primitive vocality, who would not be accepted by his fellow man, animalistic in his food and dress and yet possessing supranormal powers.

Chang would have been less than human himself if he had not acknowledged a vast curiosity to see and know this child.

The atmosphere of the swamp began to press in on him. The air was quiet. Heavy, hot fetid odors of living and decaying life, sluggishly indifferent to vagrant breezes. It was an environment, he thought, contained within itself. A muffled crash nearby startled him. Muddied water lapped violently at the dory. Looking about hastily, he saw that a skull of rock, severed from its body by the sword's edge of erosion, had slid into the water. The crash stilled for a moment the almost inaudible sibilance of chirping, snorting, grunting, a trill of grace notes in a minor key. Then the unseen wild life resumed its mating, hunting and feeding.

Chang knew a growing response to this immensely alien wilderness. It was repellent yet, in the complete absence of man, a pervading sense of the inexorable forces and spirit of nature demanded attention.

The voice of Tao, *ye, hsi, wei*—invisible, inaudible, intangible—which eludes inquiry but blends and becomes One.

Chang narrowed his eyes, scarcely breathed, tried to compress his heart's beat. What did it mean? The ephemeral condition of man, the immense vitality of life's mysteries which are divulged slowly but at the proper time?

He felt entranced, lured by the mystery, impelled

177

to seek its source, to penetrate it, to understand it. Giving way to enchantment, he picked up one of the long poles, piled near the dories. If he kept to the waterways, it would be reasonably safe. And if he should come across Christopher, perhaps Tao had decreed it.

He poled slowly, keeping always to the right, so that upon his return, by keeping to the left, he would find the entrance again. His thoughts, having been limited to problems of human behavior, plunged into a breath-taking vision of his beloved plant world. The incredible verdancy, green-shadowed, sparked with slashes of golden sunlight, surrounded him and, at times, blotted out the sky. Leaves, bushes, branches, vines, all twisting and growing in such profusion, he couldn't recall all their botanical names. The seasons, themselves, were regally ignored in this gigantic greenhouse. Spring- and fall-blooming flowers crested the high clumps of marshy earth. Pink, yellow, autumn's russet, blue, violet and red. He gave up naming them and simply rejoiced in their beauty.

There was danger, too. At every turn of the winding channel, a water snake, eeling its way through the opaque water, or the frothy wake of some underwater creature. Small rodents on the marshy shores, which froze into startled awareness of his presence, then with a dart would flee into the underbrush. Bleached bones. It was all indicative of a cruel rhythm of life which permitted the temporary intrusion of man, but would not tolerate it for long.

He had been poling for some time, and he looked for a safe place to beach the dory. He found a narrow isthmus which looked fairly firm. He pulled up the boat and squatted on his heels.

The presence of Tao, of One, was very strong.

A trickle of small pebbles startled him, somewhere up in the vine-covered crags where the far end of the spit of land joined higher ground. He turned slowly, willing himself to control any overt reaction, yet tensely prepared for attack. Rock fell again and he thought he saw a large figure scale the crag. The foliage was so dense, he could not be sure. Chang waited so long, with such absolute repose, that a chipmunk squatted near him, eating a nut. There was no further movement.

Finally he blinked, realizing he had been staring at a grove of pink azalea trees. But they were huge, twice as large as those as he had coerced into increased growth by the solution of colchicine. Without a spade and large bucket, he could not dig one up for transplanting. But behind the trees, the foliage covering the crag seemed to be an enormous strawberry vine. Chang inspected it in growing wonder. The bright green leaves were as large as his hand, and the green berries which were slowly ripening—in August?—were almost the size of apples.

Turning full circle, Chang eyed the ancient rocks with their dark crevices no eye had ever seen, subterranean rifts, extending deep into the surface of the earth, dating back to prehistoric time, through countless centuries of growth and decay. Masses of crocus and meadow saffron, blooming and dying. And depositing their unique akaloids in strata, dredged up by the seepage of swamp water. And now, it nourished this corner of the ancient greenhouse, in some form far more potent than the solution he had used as a gardening aid. There was no other explanation for the extraordinary development of the plant life in this area.

He could not transplant the azaleas, but with cuttings from the astonishing strawberry vine with its amazing fruit, he could develop a hybrid strain. He would achieve what every horticulturist dreams of—the discovery of an unknown and exotic plant, which he would name and which, his practical sense noted, would provide a source of financial support.

Packing his jacket with moist soil, he broke off

some of the twining stems and fruit, and planted them solidly, using his belt to hold the unwieldy mass together.

The sibilant sounds of the swamp grew abruptly loud with a corresponding loss of sunlight. Dusk came early in this secretive, shadowed world. Suddenly the incongruity of what he had been doing swept over him. His clothes were covered with mud, and his shoes were sodden. And with the failing of the light, his pleasure in the great greenhouse had vanished. All the troublesome reasons for being in Silverleaf returned with greater dismay and a renewed awareness of danger.

He poled rapidly with no thought for his surroundings. The rotting, heavy air had become repugnant, suffocating. When he had reached the entrance and moored the dory, he washed as effectively as he could, scraped the mud from his shoes and changed his shirt. He emptied his dufflebag and packed the strawberry vine. Carrying Luke's suitcase in the other hand, he retraced his way through the narrow entrance to the trail that would lead him to the village.

22

For the better part of an hour, Luke had traversed rough, high country through the forest north of the village. He had been forced to rely on an uncertain sense of direction. His shoes weren't suitable for walking over loose shale or climbing thrusts of rock, but the psychological hazards were harder to endure. He had never felt so alone in his life. Unidentified sounds seemed to threaten him on every side. He told himself, grimly, that identifiable sounds, a footstep or the rasp of a rifle on rock, would be infinitely more dangerous.

He stopped to catch his breath and bent to examine a minor gash on his ankle. When he straightened, the futility of what he was doing swept over him. Partially, it was the realization that in less than a week, he had been transformed from an ordinary human being, who worked and worried and accepted his lot with resignation, if not humility, into a fugitive, fleeing from the police and some evil force, conceived by Matthew Powell.

Why?

Because he never should have fled Powell's office in the first place. He should have denied all of the false insinuations, so carefully structured to implicate him, even to the money in his files. It would have been Powell's word against his.

And what if he had been subjected to a few days of humiliating interrogation? Since he intended leaving Dorn Enterprises anyway, his subsequent resignation would have been expedited. And Chang had said that much of human tragedy is caused by people disobeying the laws that regulate human behavior. Luke felt that he had been a damn fool. Law was designed to protect, not destroy. If he got a bullet in the back, it was his own fault.

Limping slightly, he continued on his hopefully correct route and, shortly, the sharply sloping slate grey roof of Vasa's lodge came into view. He was late, but Vasa's car was not there. Luke studied the open area around the lodge, screened by the thick trees. Because of him, Chang was seriously involved. And Claire, instead of fleeing to Silverleaf, should have taken the atlas and her information to someone who could have properly investigated the possibility of her son's existence. Now, how the abnormal boy could be found, induced to leave Vasa, who had obviously befriended him, and subject himself to proper medical or psychiatric treatment was beyond conjecture. The boy would never be charged with criminal intent in Groder's death. Christopher's copybook, which Luke carried in a jacket pocket, was ample evidence of what he had been subjected to. As it stood, Claire's longed-for reunion with her son depended on the uncertain motives of Vasa's devious mentality.

What could he do to rectify this senseless muddle?

The answer was obvious. When Chang came that afternoon to pick them up, he would insist they go to the nearest airport. They would not fly to another precarious refuge, but to Los Angeles to the people in charge of the Dorn investigation.

Both Claire and Chang must be induced to cooperate.

Luke was unaware of it but, instead of limping across the bricked terrace, he walked with firm, hard strides, hand raised to rap on the door. Mrs. Laroque, who had prepared their dinner the night before, must have been waiting by the wide front windows for she opened the door immediately.

"I thought you weren't coming. My husband said you left the motel early this morning. Two men stopped there. They were looking for you and her." She jerked her head toward the interior of the lodge.

"I went out early," Luke said evasively, feeling
182

his familiar cold apprehension. He frowned. The night before Mrs. Laroque had been sullenly withdrawn. Now splotches of color stained her sallow cheeks, and she tied a grey scarf around her neck with unnecessary deliberation. ''The doctor won't be coming up for lunch.''

Luke was momentarily relieved. He would be alone with Claire. Then an unpleasant possibility flashed into his mind. ''Has the doctor gone away?''

''No.'' She smiled unpleasantly. ''He's down in the village. There's been trouble.''

''What happened?''

''You'll see soon enough.''

''We're leaving in a few moments.''

Mrs. Laroque jerked her head again. ''She won't be going anyplace. She's sick.''

Claire really ill! Neither he nor Chang had foreseen this complication.

''There's sandwiches in the kitchen,'' Mrs. Laroque said. ''I won't be back.'' She pushed passed him roughly.

The bedroom door was ajar. The shades were drawn and, in the dim light, Luke saw that Claire was dressed but her limp posture was an attitude of despair and despondency. He hoped it was reaction to the stresses of the past few days, and not some serious physical affliction. But, even so, wouldn't the pathetic story in her son's copybook further distress her?

''Claire,'' he said gently.

She opened her eyes. ''Luke! Thank God, you're here. Where is that woman?''

''She left.''

Claire stood. ''The trouble with pretending to be ill is that you almost begin to believe it yourself.''

''Then you are all right?''

''I couldn't do the Venus dance, but I think so. I need to walk around.''

''And we need light in here.'' Luke pulled shades.

183

"And some lunch. Mrs. Laroque said it was in the kitchen." They left the bedroom. "What made you suspicious of Dr. Vasa?"

Claire pointed to the wall behind the stereo. "His family crest is gone. It's his most treasured possession. And it could only mean one thing. He must be intending to leave Silverleaf. But he didn't mention it last night. And then, if you remember, he didn't return my telephone calls from Los Angeles. When he comes up for lunch, I'm going to demand an explanation."

"Mrs. Laroque said he might not be coming up for lunch. There's some sort of trouble in the village."

They had reached the large main room. In the searching light from the windows, Claire raised her direct glance for a long moment. There were flecks of gold in her dark eyes. "Christopher must be the cause. The villagers' fear. The way Mrs. Laroque acted toward the doctor. My son is here somewhere. I know it. And Stefan knows."

Luke was tempted to give her the copybook and decided to wait until after lunch. First she must be convinced that the best way to save her son was by legal and medical action.

Claire suggested they take their lunch out on the terrace, have a picnic. Through the wide windows, he inspected the terrace and decided that the high, stone wall would protect them. They carried out sandwiches, a bottle of wine, a thermos of coffee and a blanket. Sun slanted through the branches of the tall pines. Its warmth created a fresh, clean pungency. Birds were chattering, flitting from tree to tree. Luke stretched out, aware of a sense of well-being for the first time in days.

Claire seemed intent on arranging their picnic when she burst out abruptly. "You've learned something, Luke. It's in your face. What is it?"

He sat up, back braced against the stone wall. She handed him a glass of wine. The copybook seemed

184

to weigh heavily in his pocket. "First I want to tell you something. Chang is here to protect us. From Sheriff Mintner. And the men who tried to kill me. Further running away is senseless."

Claire made a sound of protest.

"And. . .if your son is here, you need expert advice," he said carefully. "We must go back to Los Angeles and tell everything we know to the people in charge of the Dorn investigation."

He continued speaking of the self-critical examination experienced during his trek to the lodge, and was relieved to see her defiant expression disappear. When he had finished, she was tracing a diamond pattern on the blanket with the stem of her glass.

"I know, Luke," she said in a low voice. "I've made so many mistakes. From the time Christopher was born. I should have realized with Jasper gone there wasn't anything more to fear. Everything, the crazy job in the disco, my lies, forcing you to come here with me was because I've been alone for so long. I'd forgotten what it was like to have friends. You and Chang."

"But you did it for Christopher."

"But it was wrong. Except for loving, how could I have ever thought I'd be capable of helping him?"

"It seems we both tried to solve our problems in the wrong way. We must back up and start over. 'A journey of a thousand *li* begins at one's feet.'"

Claire smiled. "That sounds like Chang."

"It's a quotation from his favorite philosopher, Laotse. I intend to learn more. . .Claire, don't move!"

Luke flung himself forward, throwing an end of the blanket over the wriggling speckled snake which was a hand's span from her foot.

There was a simultaneous shot. Chips of grey stone splintered and flew. Claire screamed, as birds soared in a raucous cloud. Luke jerked her to her feet and streaked for the door. Two more shots shattered one

185

of the wide front windows. Shards of glass continued to fall as he slammed the door and shoved the heavy bolt in place.

"Much good it will do," he gasped. "Come on!" They ran through the large rooms. The safest place was Vasa's study. The windows were heavily shuttered, and that door was also secured with a bolt. Luke slammed the door.

They stood for a time, listening for footsteps, or any sound that would indicate further attack. They heard nothing nearby, although there was a subdued, far-off sound of shouting.

Luke looked about the room, wondering if it contained something that would provide a means of defense. The study must have also served as a consulting office. Medical supplies in a cabinet and equipment covered the inner wall. And in a corner there was a small safe. Luke knew some of what it contained. Identification papers and the money, Vasa had mentioned.

Claire sank to a chair, whispering, "When is Chang coming?"

"Soon, I hope. We'll hear his car. I wonder where they are."

"Your arm! You're hurt!"

Luke glanced down. Blood was oozing down his sleeve. Claire collected antiseptic, gauze and tape, and filled a basin with water. "Take off your jacket," she whispered angrily, and forced him toward a chair. She ripped at his shirt sleeve. "They! Who are they?"

"The guys who are trying to kill me. We think Matthew Powell is behind it. . .hey, take it easy."

She had been blotting the minor wound too vigorously. "I'm sorry."

Luke had an irrelevant thought. What would Lori have done in similar circumstances? She probably would have fainted, screamed vitriolic abuse or, perhaps, wondered if sex might save her. He marveled at the different strength flowing from Claire's now gentle fingers.

He rested his cheek against her sleek head. He should hand over Christopher's copybook. There might be only a few moments. . .and he was stuck with an anguished thought. There might be only a few moments left to both of them. There might never be a second chance for either of them in their lives. He didn't attempt to understand the rush of honest feeling. It was there and that was all that mattered.

He grasped her elbows and lifted her to her feet. "I want to tell you something more. I misjudged you from the beginning. I thought you were unstable, an unnatural mother and a selfish woman. I know now that you were constantly true to what you believed. You endured. You never lost your hope or your courage."

She looked up at him gently. Her lips quivered in a faint smile. "Since it's confession time, I'm sorry I called you a boy scout. Now, we're friends." She came into his arms. "Luke, I'm so afraid."

"So am I." He drew her to him and looked down into her gold-flecked eyes. Suddenly they kissed, passionately, with an intensity that blotted out the imminent danger.

She clung to him, whispering. "I wanted to tell you last night, when you carried me to the bedroom. I've never felt this way before. I trust you. Depend on you. You fight for what you believe."

Luke managed a smile. "After you were in bed, I sat outside in the dark, watching the lodge, and thought the same about you." He kissed her again, and felt tears on his face.

She drew back and looked at him intently. "What does it mean?"

"It means we—" He broke off. What did he have to offer her? Nothing. No family, no job and no money. Only a most uncertain future.

187

She finished his sentence. "It means we love each other. I love you, Luke."

He groaned. "God, darling—"

She kissed him. "And we share an uncertain future."

He groaned again. As if he could forget it. There in the darkened study with armed killers prowling the lodge. "Claire, I do love you. And if we ever get out of here—"

Suddenly they clung to each other, not in love, but in fear.

Footsteps!

Unsteady footsteps. Passing the door. Muted from the other rooms. Returning.

And then a low voice, "Fremont, are you in there?"

Luke shook his head, indicating silence.

"Fremont? Claire?" The voice was louder and the accent was clearly recognizable.

Luke grabbed at the bolt. "It's Vasa."

The doctor almost fell into the room. His forehead was bleeding. "Riot," he said thickly. "There's a riot in the village. I just made it. Barricade that broken window. Hurry!" His legs gave way and Luke pulled him to a chair.

"Help him," Luke told Claire. "I'll fix the window."

She cried out, "Is it safe to go out there?"

"I think so. The riot must have been the reason they didn't come after us."

Claire was kneeling, tending to Vasa's forehead. Luke looked at her briefly, tenderly. They had been granted a reprieve of sorts. He felt such an explosion of joy, he wondered that a single human being could contain it. "Claire, there's a book in my jacket pocket. But read it with relief, not regret. Afterwards, I'll tell you where Dr. Vasa went last night."

She looked up, that terrible look of hope in her eyes.

Luke nodded. "Yes, Claire. Yes. Your son is here."

188

23

The hike from the swamp to the village took a quarter of an hour. When Chang neared the rear of the motel, the sounds of angry voices, which had grown perceptibly louder, erupted into discernible words and phrases. Someone in a heavy voice called for order, but other voices clamored.

"Tell the doctor to get out of Silverleaf, Laroque." A raucous gust of jeering laughter greeted this suggestion. "No way. . .string him up. . .let's go get him now. . .where is he. . .hiding in the clinic after you beaned him. . .the son of a bitch!. . .what about what's in the swamp!"

Chang hesitated, then walked more slowly. A couple of shots exploded. As he rounded the motel and reached the main street, it was obvious that the villagers' hostility and fear was developing into mob hysteria. As yet, it had not reached a mutually acceptable course of violent action. Villagers were crowded around the front of the saloon. Liquor was being freely distributed. A number of tethered horses moved restlessly, and the barking dogs added to the confusion.

Laroque stood behind the railing of the saloon's front porch. His wife, looking like Madame Defarge, stood by him. He raised his rifle again and shot into the air. The roar of voices subsided.

He yelled, "We'd better get Vasa out here and make him explain. Then—"

A howl of derision greeted his statement. "Shit on that. . .he's been explaining for months. . .a bunch of talk. . .action, that's what we need. . .Laroque, Bow is dead. . .that thing in the swamp did it. . .Bow is dead!. . .yeah, let's burn out the swamp."

Unobserved, Chang had reached the fringes of the

crowd. The pulse of unrestrained fury and fear could be felt. A woman, standing a bit apart, looked at Chang with suspicion. He asked what had happened.

"Willie Bow was killed down on the road by a dark red car. The car was smashed to pieces."

His rented car destroyed! Chang felt a bit sick. Luke's already identified car would have to be used. If this mob didn't find it first.

The woman looked away, and Chang slipped hurriedly to the motel, circling the rear to the clinic.

Riots were not new to him. He well remembered the campus conflagrations of the sixties. And before that decade, strikes, protest groups. The mood of an angry crowd was explosive; a surging mass of undirected rage which could be sparked off in different directions by the smallest factor. But there wasn't any doubt that Dr. Vasa was one of the targets.

The back door of the clinic stood open, and Chang hastily searched the rooms. Dr. Vasa was not there. He heard footsteps at the clinic's front entrance. It would be a matter of minutes before the villagers, further angered when they found Vasa gone, would tear the clinic apart.

Regretfully Chang tossed Luke's suitcase aside, but hung on to his dufflebag. He cleared the back entrance with a leap and raced up the dirt road to the north. He didn't stop until he had reached the crest of the low hill and ducked behing a thick clump of rhododendron. He squatted down on his heels, breathing hard.

There was no question of trying to leave the village. And Luke and Claire must be warned of the impending violence. Chang hoped Vasa had already found a place to hide. And Christopher Dorn? Chang somehow felt he would be able to defend himself.

There were growing sounds of destruction from the clinic. Chang headed north where Luke had said the lodge was, but behind the trees that fringed the road.

If the two hunters were lurking nearby, Chang wasn't taking any chances.

In the large main room of the lodge, a highboy was shielding the broken window; all the other windows had been barricaded with furniture and blankets. Rifle at hand, Luke sat on the floor by a sliver of space between the highboy and the window frame. He could see the road clearly for at least a quarter of a mile which would give them some advance warning, in the event the villagers appeared. The stone lodge could not be ignited and, with another man at the back to watch, Luke felt an attack could be held off for some time. If only Chang would show up.

"Here's coffee," Claire said, coming into the room. She placed a mug on the floor by Luke. The copybook was under her arm. She bent and pressed her cheek to his.

He kissed her. "How's the doctor?"

"Still pretty muddled."

"Has he said anything about Christopher?"

"No. He must have had a terrible blow to the side of his head. But he managed to call the Forestry Service again. The men are still out fighting that fire in a nearby canyon. They promised to come as soon as possible."

She sank to the floor and rested her head against his shoulder. "Somehow I don't feel afraid anymore."

"I'm glad."

"But Christopher? Luke, what will happen to him?"

"Claire, you must have read the copybook a dozen times. According to what he wrote, he's strong and capable. If it comes to a physical confrontation, he can handle himself."

She fell silent for a time. Then she repeated a question she had asked countless times. "Why? Oh God, why Gil and me? How could I have given birth to him? Thousands of children are born every minute all over the world. Why?"

"I don't know. Perhaps Vasa can explain when he recovers. He's had about six months to study the boy."

"The brutal treatment. What he must have suffered. When I think about it, I—"

"Don't think about it," Luke said sharply "People always fear the unknown, and try to destroy what they don't understand."

"I've got to see him. Try to explain."

"Claire, he wrote that journal more than six months ago. Perhaps, through Vasa, his ideas have changed. He has learned trust."

"Where do you suppose Stefan was planning to take him?"

"I don't know." But Luke felt a greater dismay, remembering the overheard talk in the swamp. To a place where Christopher could run naked, hunt and fish, eat his kind of food, and live life on his terms.

"Claire, look! Isn't that Chang behind the trees to the left of the road?"

"Yes. It is!"

"Wait until he reaches the door, then I'll open it quickly."

Shortly Chang was in the lodge, considerably winded. He grinned. "So you're still alive."

Luke pounded his shoulder. "What's going on down there?"

"The cloud is still forming. But the deluge could explode anyplace. I couldn't find the doctor."

"He's been hurt. He's here."

At that moment from the couch in his study, Vasa pushed up on an elbow. His voice sounded quite normal. "Claire, will you bring the green capsules on the second shelf in the medicine cabinet? I need a stimulant." His detached manner had left him, to be replaced by haggard lines and shadows of pain and fatigue around his eyes and mouth. "Have the villagers been up here?"

"No. Not yet," Chang said. Vasa looked at him indifferently.

Claire handed the doctor the capsules he had requested. "Stefan, you lied. Christopher is here. I want the truth."

Vasa began. "My dear, this is hardly the time or the place—"

"But the time and the place couldn't be more suitable. Stefan, if you don't tell us, when that mob comes up the road, you will be waiting for it. Alone, on the terrace."

Vasa looked at her for a long moment. An expression of malevolent admiration crossed his face. The roar from the village grew louder. With difficulty, he swallowed two capsules. "Those ignorant fools! Mired in the mud of their own stupidity. All right! What do you want me to tell you? The boy is here. He has been here for more than six months." Something of his superior, sardonic manner returned to him. "Do you realize, my dear Claire, you gave birth to an individual who might be the salvation of the human race in the 21st century!"

Claire gasped. Chang and Luke exchanged a look which expressed their mutual doubt about Vasa's sanity.

The noise from the village was explosive.

Vasa lurched to his feet and shrugged off Chang's supportive hand. He muttered something in his native Hungarian. And then he lapsed into English. "We must save him. My God, yes, save him."

24

Vasa reached the main room and moved unsteadily to the liquor cabinet. He poured a straight drink which he swallowed in a single gulp. His scarred hands were trembling. The man was possessed by anxiety. Not for himself, but for Christopher. He shuddered with each explosive sound from the village.

Luke knelt at his lookout; Claire sat near him. Chang said in a low voice, they had better not snap on any lights, even though it was almost night. But he placed his lighted flashlight on the mantel over the wide fireplace, and its glow illuminated the room faintly.

Vasa turned, a humorless slash of a smile in his lined face. "There isn't time to relate the results of the medical and psychological procedures I employed over the last months to test Christopher. But the safe in my study contains two tape recordings which verify my conclusions, as far as I was able to go without more sophisticated equipment."

"Why were you planning to take him somewhere? To test him further?" Luke said over his shoulder.

"Yes. How did you know that?"

"I followed you to the swamp last night. I overheard you. Where were you going?"

"Does it matter now? It was all arranged. An isolated refuge where I could continue my work. God, it can't end like this."

Another burst of gunfire was heard. "If those fools go to the swamp—"

"Doctor," Chang broke in quickly, "tell us and then we can decide what to do."

Vasa swallowed another drink and began rapidly. "In late March a road maintainance crew came upon a nearly nude boy, lying in a ditch by the side of the road. There had been a heavy snowstorm, but the boy was alive, warm and sleeping peacefully. I was informed and instructed the men to bring him to the clinic. But when they returned to where he had been found, he had disappeared. About a week later, early morning, I was awakened by a sound in my bedroom. A naked young man stood in a corner. I was able to grasp a few words of his unintelligible speech. He told me his name was Christopher Dorn and he had a disease which he wanted me to study.''

Luke drew Claire to his side. She was pale and trembling.

"We began to communicate through printing. At first, I accepted the earlier diagnoses he described. Acromegaly. A genetic defect of the pituitary. But I began to recognize that he had a superior intelligence. And he was not a human freak as he had been led to believe. In the last two months, his rapid growth has considerably lessened. He is almost seven feet tall. His head, which had grown rapidly after birth to accommodate an adult brain, and his extremities are not now excessively large. I believe he has reached physical and mental maturity.''

"But he's only a child,'' Claire cried. "Almost six. How could it have happened? What caused it?''

"A genetic mutation must have occurred. I don't know why. That is what I intend to discover. And I will! You will find it even more difficult to accept when I describe the powers he possesses. Claire, do you remember Nurse Reed?''

"Yes. She was the special RN who came from Boise for two weeks when my son was born.''

"She told me of an eerie incident which occurred during her first night on duty. She was checking on the two infants in the nursery. The night light had burned out and, before she could find another, she heard a whispering, like a rush of water in a narrow channel. Christopher was whispering your name, my name, the names of his father, the nurse, the village.''

"Why can't he speak now?" Chang asked.

"Possibly his incredibly rapid development impaired the growth of his vocal apparatus. But I am more inclined to believe that this inability to speak was due to imitative behavior. His vocal chords atrophied."

Claire gasped brokenly. "I used to beg him not to speak. To be a normal baby."

"Yes, he wrote of that. At the time I thought Nurse Reed was nervous. The mountainous environment was alien to her. I thought she had imagined the incident. But through the tests, I learned that Christopher, as an infant, was able to think, reason, deduce, perceive, plan, and he could have vocalized all of this. He remembers every detail of his life from the moment he first drew breath. He knows his father tried to kill him."

Luke turned from his lookout. "Claire, is that true?"

"Yes," she said in a low voice.

Vasa began to pace the room. "His incarceration and brutal treatment by an orderly in the nursing home further convinced him of his differences. The confinement to which he was subjected was torture because his rapidly growing body needed movement and exercise. He planned his escape in every detail. His chance meeting with the members of the commune deflected his purpose for a time which was to come to me for explanation of why he was called a freak. A young woman in the commune, named Lily, became a protector of sorts, but she was unable to prevent further brutal treatment. He was indoctrinated in criminal activity because of his superior physical powers but, in all other respects, he was a prisoner, subjected to torture and confinement again. Hence, his second escape."

"Why didn't you contact Claire when he came here?" Luke asked.

Vasa ignored the question. "I have learned that

physically he is impervious to pollution or contagion and infection. He does not feel excessive heat or cold. His body receives nourishment from foods that our ancestors might have eaten, raw flesh and indigestible grains. He possesses strengths and endurance far beyond the norm. He has highly acute senses. He is able to direct the body's healing defenses to source of disfunction, thereby curing it. It is a paradox that probably in some earlier stage of human development, man possessed some of these qualities. He is, in a sense, tuned in to these earlier abilities and, at the same time, possesses a stable mentality that does not exist in our present evolution. He does not experience anxiety, guilt, neuroses, emotional extremes, which are psychosomatic causes of organic decay and mental aberration. He does not know love, hate or fear as we do. He does not lie. He has had a set of moral standards from birth. And yet it is a simple morality."

Vasa was becoming extremely agitated. He was breathing rapidly and cringed each time there were noises from the village.

"He is a perfectly functioning organism, designed for one purpose only. To survive."

"Survive?" Luke stared. "But I gathered from your talk with him in the swamp, his life is in danger."

"Here, under present conditions, yes. But envision a hundred years from now. Perhaps after a nuclear war. Death, devastation, disease, famine. Overpopulation, shortages of food, water, clothing, habitation. With our frailties, we are doomed. But Christopher would survive."

Claire uttered a faint scream. "His feet. The thickened skin. He doesn't need shoes."

"Probably early man didn't either. Yes, he can run for miles over rocky terrain that would cripple us."

Vasa moved his head uneasily. There were no shouts or shots to be heard from the village. It was ominously still.

"The most remarkable fact of all," he said hoarsely, "is the length of his gestation period. Instead of nine months, I believe it was half that time. It is a revolutionary cycle of birth. And he subsequently achieved maturity in five years instead of a decade and a half, thereby enormously reducing early years of helpless and harmful dependence. I believe he is the first of a vastly superior species."

Vasa studied their startled faces. "Have none of you grasped it? Don't you understand? His children and children's children will form a new race of men. Men who will truly inherit the earth."

Chang said something in Chinese. It sounded like a prayer. Luke caught the word Tao.

Vasa laughed sickly. "The Nazis tried to achieve an Aryan ideal through breeding. I always believed the idea was insane. Now I know, through a genetic miracle, Christopher represents that ideal. He is that ideal."

"And that's why you didn't contact Claire. And it's also the reason why you didn't take him to a medical center for study and observation. You wanted to be the power behind. . .this miracle," Chang said.

"Yes!" Vasa shouted. He was about to continue when he stared at the wide windows. At one side of a draped blanket, there was a sliver of light, growing brighter. "Oh God, they've gone to the swamp." He jerked one of the blankets down. In the dark expanse of wilderness, they could see a wide, smoky pool of fire.

Vasa was already collecting flashlights. "I must go to him."

"He could be killed," Claire cried out. "Luke and Chang, you must go with the doctor."

"And leave you here alone?" Luke said. "No."

"I'll be all right. I'll lock myself in the study. Go on. Hurry!" She thrust sweaters at them and saw them to the back entrance of the lodge.

25

They followed the dark rutted road to the north, the same route Vasa had taken the night before. But this time they moved with frantic haste, Vasa stopping a number of times to rest and, it seemed, to listen. Once he called out cautiously for Christopher, but there was no answer. When they reached the unmarked trail to begin the downward climb, their rough descent was illuminated by murky, fitful light. Shots rang out frequently, and the villagers could be heard, hooting and shouting. By the time Chang and Luke, slipping and sliding, had reached the narrow ledge, jutting over the deep black pool of water, Vasa had already vanished. But they heard his peremptory order, "There isn't adequate space. Wait there."

Squatting on the ledge, Luke and Chang could see a portion of the swamp. It could have been a scene out of Dante's *Inferno*. Spotty fires and smoldering, billowing smoke wafted and surged. Some of the men carried flaming torches. Others in dories were poling, fanning out in an attempt to investigate the branching waterways.

"They haven't gotten in very far," Luke said in a low voice. "But we'd better turn off our flashlights."

"Quiet," Chang said. "Listen."

There was the slap-splash of a pole near their position and, seen through the foliage in the uncertain light, a dory with two men was angling into a nearby channel.

"Maybe we'd better wait for the others," one of the men said.

"No. Just keep your eyes open," the other replied. "Use your flash."

Chang and Luke inched to the V end of the ledge and pressed against the rocky wall as a narrow beam of light played along the rim. Luke swore softly when Vasa's voice could be heard, calling for the boy.

"Hold it," one of the men said. "I heard something." The dory came to a sluggish stop on the bank of the channel.

"Christopher? Are you there, Christopher?" Vasa's voice could be clearly heard.

"We've got to warn him," Chang whispered.

"We can't. I don't know where the damn entrance is."

There was a hoarse, mewling snarl.

"You must save yourself," Vasa said urgently. "Go. Go now!"

The answering moan was unmistakably negative. It was followed by what seemed to be a series of angry questions.

"It has nothing to do with you, Christopher. They don't know what they're doing."

Another question.

"Kill you?" Vasa echoed, uncertainty ragged in his voice. "God, yes! They want to kill you. Don't risk your life. Run. Save yourself!" Vasa broke into an incoherent entreaty, some of it in Hungarian.

The men in the dory reacted with excited fear. "It sounds like the doctor."

"Yeah, but what about—"

Vasa was screaming. "For God's sake, get out of here!"

Luke and Chang heard the thud and crash of sudden movement. A large figure erupted out of the darkness. It leaped by them with such force that Luke, who was the nearer, staggered under a hard thrust and only Chang's steadying hold kept him from falling forward into the black pool.

One of the men shouted, "Someone just went up the face of the embankment!"

At that moment, from below, Vasa began climbing

to the ledge. Chang and Luke knelt, ready to help him. Shots exploded. Vasa's scarred hands clawed at the rim of eroded rock. Then he fell backward, with a splashing crash, into the dark water below.

"I think we got something," one of the men yelled.

Luke and Chang peered down. Vasa was floating on his back, arms outspread. Then he sank out of sight. A few eddying bubbles erupted on the surface of the black water.

The men in the dory began to argue about searching immediately or waiting until morning. A heightened outcry could be heard at the entrance to the swamp.

"Jeeze," one of the men said. "It's the forest rangers. We'd better get out of here."

Chang and Luke waited until the dory was some distance away. Then they inched their way on the ledge to the trail where they could climb to higher ground.

During the long hike back to the lodge, the men rarely spoke. There was no need to exchange their thoughts; they were too similar. Christopher was running wild and free. Where? Claire, waiting and hoping, would suffer another devastating disappointment. And Dr. Stefan Vasa, in his determination to study and to dominate, to exploit the power which he had hoped to achieve, had subscribed to the very evil that had twisted and distorted his own life and, in the end, it had brought him death.

26

The first light of dawn filled the main room in Vasa's lodge. Except for forest sounds, the world was silent again. Luke, who had just opened the bolted shutters, began pulling at the blankets and furniture covering the windows. Claire was helping Chang loosen some of the tangled vines of the strawberry plant in his dufflebag.

"May I eat a berry, Chang?" she asked.

Chang and Luke exchanged a glance. Her interest in anything, even berries, was a hopeful indication that she was recovering from the waxen immobility of the past hour. There had been no tears, no hysteria, which might have helped. Only a plaintive, broken moaning when she was told what had happened in the swamp.

"The berries remind me of the picnic Gil and I had with Sara and Bob." She swallowed and tried to steady her voice. "You must have found the same spot we did."

Chang looked up. "A narrow spit of fairly solid land in the channel on the right?"

Claire nodded. Abruptly she crumpled and sank to a chair, covering her eyes. "If only you could have stopped him!"

Luke knelt by her. "There was no way we could have. He appeared so quickly and disappeared in less time than it takes to speak about it."

"And if he hadn't escaped, those men in the dory—" Chang began.

"I'm not blaming either of you. But to have come so near to finding him—"

Chang said hastily. "What time did the rangers arrive?"

"An hour or more, after you left for the swamp. They wanted to talk to Stefan and learn what had caused the riot. They decided they'd better stop the shooting and the fires, and left immediately. Poor Stefan. Do you think they've found him?"

"They will, sooner or later," Luke said, wondering how the villagers would explain Vasa's death.

"And what about Christopher? What should we do? Tell the rangers and ask them to search for him?"

Luke frowned. "No, Claire. It would have to be a search with dogs and guns. He might be killed."

"But the villagers. They'll tell about him," Claire pointed out.

"I don't think so," Chang said. He had moved to the windows and was studying the road. "Vasa's death has to be explained. We know the villagers intended to kill your son and the doctor. But if they insist that the reason they were burning out the swamp was to rid the village of marauding animals, then Vasa's death is accidental."

"And if the rangers hear stories about someone living in the swamp, there's no evidence to involve Christopher in any of it." Luke shook Claire gently. "Come on, darling, don't look so unhappy."

She looked up with a bitter smile. "How could my son be involved? His grave is in the Dorn family plot. I suppose I should thank Jasper for that, too."

"Stop regretting the past, Claire." Chang said firmly. "You should be thinking about the future. If Vasa's conclusions were correct, your son does represent an evolutionary change. We must open the safe and take his tapes, and they must be given to experts in order to discover how this extraordinary change occurred."

Claire nodded. "But with no publicity. No TV. No reporters." She stood and walked to the windows. "He's out there somewhere," she said softly. "And we'll find him.'' She turned in sudden concern. ''What if he leaves this area?''

''Why should he?'' Luke said. ''There are miles and miles of uninhabited land. Mountains, rivers to explore.''

All three of them looked at the wide expanse of forest. Except for slender spirals of black smoke from the swamp, the brown and green verdancy stretched unbroken to a mountainous blue horizon.

Claire turned from the window. Faint color had returned to her face. ''I somehow feel very humble. And ashamed, too. You've been worrying about my problems. And not giving a thought to yours.'' She intended to raid the kitchen and find something for an early breakfast.

The men waited until they heard the sound of cupboard doors opening and shutting. ''And problem number one is,'' Luke said, ''how in the hell are we going to get out of Silverleaf?''

''Go down to the village, as soon as we can. Explain that we spent a terrified night in the doctor's lodge. Find your rented car, hopefully intact, and take off.''

''What about those two supposed hunters? I haven't had a chance to tell you. They tried again yesterday, and failed.''

Chang nodded. ''With the Forestry Service in the village, I don't think we need worry about that. What I'm more concerned about is Sheriff Mintner. He could arrive any minute.''

''It doesn't make any difference. Claire and I are going back to LA anyway. All she has to do is identify herself and stick to her story; she was not told about what happened in the nursing home and there is her son's grave to support her story. I'll have a great deal more to explain. But I can take it.''

Chang nodded again, sighing. ''I can see that the two of you are beginning a journey together. But I am nearing the end of mine, perhaps only to find that I took the wrong path after all."

It was so unlike Chang to admit to defeat. Luke assumed he was referring to the suspension and his ravaged greenhouse. But his regret went far deeper than that.

"I never questioned Western beliefs and attitudes. They are sometimes ruthless and crude, but they are growing. But I am Chinese, Luke. In the East, a man or woman who has lived a productive life is regarded with respect and honor. Those qualities are more important than the fame and fortune you Westerners desire so avidly. I will return to Los Angeles with you and Claire where I face shame and failure."

Luke had never heard a personal revelation that was more dismaying. "God, Chang, I'll explain what happened. Take your own advice. No regrets. Apply some creative thought to Matthew Powell and—"

"I need some help," Claire called out. She was carrying a heavy tray. Luke took it from her. She saw their somber faces. "Let's declare a moratorium," she said, passing around plates and mugs. "Or have we forgotten how to share an idle conversation."

They heard a wrenching crash in the study. Chang reached for his revolver. Claire, who was still standing, moved quickly to the study door. She stood there for an endless moment. Then she uttered a heart-shuddering scream.

"Christopher!"

The men darted to the door.

"Christopher!"

An indistinct figure was crouched by the safe. Its door had been pulled away. Two boxes of tape recordings and other papers littered the floor.

"Christopher. Son!"

He straightened and stood tensely. Except for a jock strap, he was nude. A body, broad shouldered and

205

graceful, with long athletic legs. A sculptured head. A fall of heavy pale hair around a wide forehead. His eyes were dark-fringed and piercingly blue. His classic features could have created another David for Michelangelo.

He was the most superbly beautiful human being any of them had ever seen.

Claire took a step forward. "I'm Claire. I'm your mother."

Christopher backed away, raising his long, powerful arms in a defensive attitude. He was holding a passport and a packet of papers in one hand. In the other was a thick sheaf of money.

Claire took another step. "Listen to me. Can you understand. I've loved you all of these years. I love you now, and I want to help you."

The dark blue eyes widened with comprehension, then darted toward the men.

Claire stepped forward again. "They are my friends. They want to help, too."

Christopher's eyes moved back to her, and his lips moved with a flash of white teeth. He said in a hoarse choked whisper, "Mother?"

"Yes. Your mother."

Luke and Chang said nothing, fearing to startle him.

Claire held up her arms. "Come. Kiss me. Let me hold you. I have your book. I know what you suffered—"

A heavy pounding of feet could be heard, crossing the terrace. There was a rapid knock on the front door. "Open up!"

Christopher looked warily toward the source of the noise.

"Open up in there!"

Faintly frowning, Christopher looked steadily at Claire. His lips moved soundlessly, as he took a single step forward. He whirled and disappeared through one of the study windows.

"Christopher!" Claire screamed and sagged limply. Luke caught her. Chang darted forward and scooped up the two boxes of tape recordings. In the main room he thrust them into the dufflebag and went to the front door.

A uniformed Sheriff Mintner charged in, flanked by two plainclothesmen. "Chang, I might have known you'd be here." He pushed Chang aside, eyes searching the room. "Fremont. And Claire Dorn." Nodding with satisfaction, he fumbled in a jacket pocket for an envelope.

"Luke Fremont. You are under arrest and will be escorted back to Los Angeles for questioning about the murder of Jasper Dorn."

There was a flash of dangling handcuffs as one of the detectives moved forward.

Mintner smiled broadly. "Looks like you people picked the wrong place to hide out. There must have been some dust-up last night. Place is crawling with state police. Half the village is arrested for destruction of government land. A Dr. Vasa was killed in the confusion, and two guys after deer were injured, trying to leave the village. Without extradition papers, you would have been identified and sent back to L.A. anyway."

27

The fabled California sun, diffused by the equally famous smog, shone dully behind slatted blinds which encircled the windowed room. Not a courtroom, Luke saw with dulled perception. But a conference room; three long tables with hard chairs, grouped carelessly. The room was nearly empty. Two court clerks gossiped in low voices; and three men with briefcases, possibly Dorn's personal attorneys, stared at him with ill-concealed curiosity.

Luke's guard indicated that he was to sit at the far table, and he sagged to a hard chair, hands pressed to his throbbing head. He had been questioned in the county jail all morning and had been given a statement to sign. He had eaten lunch from a tray, under the watchful eyes of his guard.

There had been an air of secrecy, of unreality, from the moment of his arrest, and during the flight to Los Angeles. He had been taken to a motel room, which had no television or radio. In the morning, he had been given clothes and shoes, obviously new but ill-fitting. He had shaved off his growth of beard, but there was nothing he could do about his untidy, dark hair. And now, he was in the civil, not criminal, division of the county courthouse. The car, transporting him, had entered the building through a back entrance of a subterranean garage.

Luke assumed the reason for the irregular proceedings arose out of the necessity to avoid undue publicity until depositions had been taken and formal charges made.

His interrogation, although tedious, had not been unpleasant. Without any reference to Christopher Dorn, he had explained the week's erratic flight was the result of an attempt to avoid false arrest. Strangely enough, he had not been asked why he had gone to Silverleaf, Montana, with Claire Dorn. Or if he knew why she had changed her name and had not contacted authorities. For some unexplained reason, there had been countless questions about the orphanage and his childhood years. But most of the questions had centered on his activities on the Friday night when Jasper Dorn was murdered and the unexplainable ten thousand dollars found in his files. He had not revealed Matthew Powell's role in inducing him to flight. But, if and when Luke was brought to trial, he intended that Powell and his furtive plot would form the basis of his defense. Chang would back him up about the shots on the nursing home grounds. And Sara Brown and Bob Fairway would testify about the explosive in his car.

There was a flurry of movement at the door, and Luke turned hoping to see Claire and Chang. Two people entered. An ancient black woman, escorted by a black man about Luke's age. They smiled and nodded as they found seats at the second table.

Time passed; a fly buzzed. Luke was more struck with the air of unreality. It seemed they were all actors on a stage and only he didn't know his role.

Of one thing, he was dead certain. If this day were an indication of what the future might be, his life would become one undeniable hell. Regret, that self-defeating emotion, had taken possession of him. What would happen to the love that he and Claire had so belatedly shared? What if he were sent to prison and they were to be separated for months, years? And, if and when he was eventually freed to pick up the tattered shreds of his career, wouldn't the stigma of his disgrace destroy any possibility of a life together?

The two clerks terminated their conversation abruptly and sat down by the three other men. An air of expectancy seemed to fill the room. Luke looked toward the door. Claire was standing there, hesitantly. She was transformed. He had never seen her wear anything but jeans and a shirt, or that parody of a sex costume, and now, in a pale beige pants suit, her long dark hair gleaming, she looked inexpressably lovely. Luke was swept with an aching yearning to hold her in his arms.

Their eyes met, and she immediately glanced away. Then he saw who was behind her, guiding her across the room to his table. Matthew Powell! Luke sat back, tense with shock. The baffling web of his inexplicable involvement was unbearable. When they reached his table, the expectant silence in the room made any sort of a greeting impossible. They sat down silently. Luke stared at her serene profile in disbelief. Beyond her, Powell, looking gaunt but impeccably groomed, focussed his attention on the mottled table top. Luke resisted the impulse to jump to his feet, or shout and run, do anything to relieve his dismay.

A last arrival entered from a side door and sat alone at the main table. She was a small, plump woman with greying hair, wearing a smart purple pants suit. She polished her glasses vigorously as one of the clerks plumped a sheaf of blue-encased depositions on the table in front of her.

The clerk announced in a bored voice, "Judge Josephine B. Davis."

Judge Davis, glasses on her nose, looked about the room and nodded, as if assuring herself that everyone was present. She cleared her throat and spoke in a rapid and unexpectedly deep voice. "As you may have gathered, this is an informal meeting of concerned parties since no unlawful action is involved. But the extraordinary circumstances seemed to require some sort of legal direction."

She hesitated for a moment. "First of all, Mr. Fremont, the court wishes to extend an apology. The all-points bulletin which was issued for your arrest should have been later withdrawn. But a number of facts had to be verified and, as it developed, you were a difficult person to locate. You have not been formally booked, and there has been no announcement to the press.''

In tones of quiet fury, Luke asked, ''Then why am I here?''

''That will be explained shortly. First of all, these statements have completely clarified a number of un-warranted assumptions and suspicions.'' She pushed the depositions aside.

Judge Davis looked at Claire. ''In that respect, Mrs. Dorn, although a change of name could be considered an extreme measure in an effort to maintain privacy regarding the tragic events in your life, the controversy on TV and in the press about your incurably ill son, based on the questionable identification of two motorists, is to be deplored. May the child rest in peace.''

Luke found he couldn't look at Claire. Whatever else she had compromised, she was a mother to the very end. Christopher's staged internment in the Dorn family plot had effectively eliminated any suspicion that he was alive.

Judge Davis studied a typewritten sheet of paper. ''Since everyone present has been involved in the investigation of the death of Jasper Dorn, I think it is reasonable and fair to reveal that his assailant and murderer is a man who is, at the moment, in custody. Local and federal authorities will release his name and relevant information at the proper time.''

As if he were a puppet on a string, Luke turned in his chair and stared at Matthew Powell. Except for a bunching of muscles on the line of his jaw, Powell did not react. He did not seem impressed or even particularly interested.

Chang had it all wrong! Dorn's death was not part

211

of Powell's plan to discredit him, Luke thought with despair. But if someone had been arrested, that let him off the hook.

"And now, Mr. Fremont," Judge Davis said. "The explanation due you is forthcoming. Mr. Powell, perhaps you would care to elucidate further."

Powell rose slowly but didn't look at Luke. "Yes, your honor. The money found in Mr. Fremont's office files was put there by mistake. That particular folder had been on Mr. Dorn's desk just before we left for Washington. I knew that he had been withdrawing large amounts of cash for about six months. It has been established that he was being blackmailed, although the reason is not known. This sum must have been another payment. Perhaps he had wished to conceal such a large sum from an unexpected visitor and had thrust it in the folder. While we were in Washington, my assistant, seeing that the folder carried the red research tag, top secret, put it in Mr. Fremont's files. I regret the unfortunate oversight, but then we were all very upset by Mr. Dorn's death." Powell sat down.

Judge Davis nodded. "Do you wish to say anything, Mr. Fremont?"

"No." Luke's silent fury had deepened. It was to be expected that Powell would find a way to save himself, to conceal why he had forced Luke into the spot light of suspicion. For the first time Claire looked directly at Luke. She was smiling. Smiling! Didn't she realize Powell was lying?

Judge Davis continued. "Mr. Fremont, there was a reason why, for a time, you were the primary suspect, the person responsible for Mr. Dorn's death. Due to tax problems, a federal injunction ordered the reading of Mr. Dorn's will, prior to the time all of his beneficiaries had been notified. In line with the personal motive theory the investigators were pursuing, it was also hoped that Mr. Dorn's will would provide some clue to his murderer. The will revealed that you had a motive which seemed conclusive.''

"I had a motive!" Luke choked.

"Yes. It is quite in line with what we know of Mr. Dorn's character, his insistence on propriety and his reticence about his personal life.'' Judge Davis cleared her throat. "His will clearly states that you are his natural and unacknowledged son. You are the principal beneficiary of his personal fortune and will also inherit controlling interest in Dorn Enterprises.''

The dizziness Luke felt was a warning that he was about to drop to the floor in a dead faint. He was saved by the sharp edge of the table as he sagged forward. He raised his head when he heard a soft melodic voice.

"Don't you remember me, Luke?'' It was the aged black woman. "I cared for you after your mother passed away at your birth. When you were two years old, Mr. Dorn took you away.''

The young black man shook Luke's hand. "Don't you remember how we used to swim at the lake?''

Luke closed his eyes. The tag end of the memory that had often occupied his thoughts and recently when he was sitting in the Hollywood park fell into remembered focus.

"Yes," he said unsteadily. "You're Percy. And you are Mrs. Eilers.''

They nodded, and everyone began to talk at once.

Dazedly, Luke glanced at the expressions on the encircling ring of faces. The clerks were staring with envy. Judge Davis, benevolently. There were tears in Claire's eyes. Luke felt hot shame that he could have ever doubted her. But his sense of incredulity deepened.

"I can't believe it—" he began. No one heard him. Everyone was talking more loudly. The three attorneys were attempting to reach him. ". . .reading of the will. . .papers to sign."

And then Luke saw Powell's grim, dark face. And incredulity vanished. Powell's face was furrowed with the sick lines of defeat. Luke could accept the unbelievable fact that he was Jasper Dorn's son. Powell had known it and had stooped to murder. Dorn Enterprises was the prize.

Luke smiled, and Powell turned away. His fists were clenched.

Judge Davis called out sharply. "Please, please sit down. I insist on silence. This is not a court of law but some decorum is necessary." The noise subsided. "Accept my congratulations, Luke Fremont Dorn. There is nothing more to discuss. Except for a suggestion. Since I am releasing this information to the press, I would advise that all of you retire to a secluded place where you will be relatively safe from journalistic zeal." The judge left the room.

Powell stood heavily and departed without a word.

Luke reached for Claire. They exchanged a jumble of words that neither of them heard. Finally Luke asked, "Where shall we go?"

"To Chang's." Claire blew her nose. "He's expecting us."

28

The impromptu gathering had been interrupted twice by reporters. Chang dealt with them in the patio of his home in Belden Beach. The press, intent on tracking down rumors that the Dorn murder had been solved, were further frustrated since Chang knew nothing. After the second invasion, he locked the front door and announced that from now on there would be no further interruptions. No one paid much attention. Hilda Beck was helping Bob Fairway chill champagne. Claire and Jade were conferring about dinner in the kitchen. Luke was glancing through a stack of Dorn Enterprises policy papers. And Sara Brown was sitting cross-legged on the floor, eyes half-closed behind her round glasses and hands on her knees.

Early that morning Chang had contacted Claire. Knowing the clamor the announcement of Luke's heritage and inheritance would cause, he had offered his home as a refuge. It was Claire who had suggested the inclusion of the others. The evening promised to be calm and quiet, the first in many days.

Chang stretched out in his favorite chair. The past twenty-four hours had been a period of extraordinary events, his own situation among them. Upon landing at L.A. International, he had been whisked to police headquarters in Monterey County. And Sheriff Marc Mintner. Mintner had not apologized, but he had brusquely acknowledged his errors. In the light of subsequent events, Chang's suspension, the suspicion of sexual irregularity and aiding and abetting a wanted man were no longer pertinent. His retirement on full pension was not threatened. "The slate's clean," Mintner had rasped. "How about another tour of duty? I've got a couple of good openings."

Chang had been contemplating the restoration of his greenhouse and the cultivation of the hybrid strawberry vine and had asked that he be permitted to complete his vacation—there were almost three weeks to go—to think it over. He had been driven home, collecting Jade at his cousin's en route.

That morning he had enjoyed his early morning swim, realizing that when extraordinary events occur, it is wise to adhere to the routine of one's days. Otherwise, perspective will be lost. Stroking around the length of the pier, he saw that the *Sea Lion* was gone and a phone call to Barker at the substation had elicited a terse. . .who cares? Captain Leo Stone was probably nursing a beer in some coastal Mexican town, wondering if Chang had revealed that it had been he who had moved Jasper Dorn's body to the grounds of the nursing home. Chang hadn't and never would. Let Mintner figure it out. But Chang sighed. He had been guilty of gross errors, too. Although Matthew Powell had certainly been responsible for L. Avery Boyd's accident at the gate house and the attacks on Luke in order to take over Dorn Enterprises, he had not killed Dorn, according to Mintner's offensively superior announcement that the Dorn case had been solved. And Chang had been mistaken in thinking that the evil seed planted by Dorn's death would blossom into malignancy. Even so, the lives of each of them had been vastly altered.

Chang sighed again. The direction of his life had been changed, too, and it was imperative that he decide what to do.

Sara uttered a prolonged, "Ohmmmmm." At the same time the cork on the first bottle of champagne popped. It was a minor salute to the beginning of their party, Chang thought, but he was mistaken. Sara sat up alertly and began studying everyone with a relentlessly curious expression.

"Now, Luke," she began, "do you mean to say that you had no idea you were J.D.'s illegitimate son?"

"Sara!" Bob protested.

"Absolutely not," Luke said somberly. "But, now, of course, some things seem so evident. I went through prep school and college on convenient and substantial scholarships. And I was offered a job with Dorn Enterprises even before I graduated. What I believed where lucky breaks must have been arranged by. . .him."

Luke had not found a way to refer to Jasper Dorn, even in his thoughts.

"And he was always so interested in what I thought. My work and a great many problems that weren't connected with my work." Luke closed his eyes.

"Now that you're boss," Sara asked, "what are you doing to do about that leper, Matthew Powell?"

Luke didn't hear the question. He was remembering with minute accuracy the hand-written portion of Jasper Dorn's last will and testament.

"It is regretable that my second son, Gilbert, would never have become a responsible man. In any event, his self-imposed death rendered inheritance impossible. My grandson, Christopher, would never have been capable of assuming leadership. I have provided for Claire Dorn, my daughter-in-law, in the hope that the future security will compensate for her tragic association with the Dorn family.

"I name my first son, Luke Fremont, my legal heir. His mother, Mary Fremont, was a loving, honest woman who refused to accept my offer of marriage. By temperament and character, she was unwilling to become a part of the life I had always pursued. I have grown to recognize that there are qualities in me that she tolerated but could not live with. But I never doubted her love for me. Her loss was the first and most despairing event of my life. I vowed I would direct and nurture the course of our son's life and career. I know Mary's last act of loving kindness was to have given me a son worthy of assuming the heavy responsibilities that Enterprises will place upon his shoulders. When the proper time comes, I will tell him. But, until then, I cannot permit the slightest possibility that Enterprises might fall into the hands of associates who, for personal and avaricious reasons, would destroy Enterprises.

"If and when this will is read, except for listed bequests, my personal assets and the controlling interest in Dorn Enterprises are the sole possession of Luke Fremont Dorn."

Luke opened his eyes and looked at Sara. "What did you say?"

"Are you going to fire Powell?"

Luke considered the possibility for a moment, revealing the objectivity and audacity that he would one day exert. "At the moment, I don't think so. Powell fought for what he wanted, and he lost. But that doesn't diminish his importance to Enterprises. In fact, I anticipate that our relationship will be quite amicable."

Sara shuddered. "God, you sound like J.D. I hope you're not going to become a chip off the old boulder."

Luke laughed. "No danger of that. There are no secrets between Claire and me."

"But there are a few mysteries." Claire laughed, too, as she entered the room. "I don't know what kind of salad dressing you like."

"There's lots of time to find out."

Sara jumped to her feet. "Please, don't get off the subject. What are you going to do about your name? I mean, aren't they both Dorn now? You don't even have to get married."

Luke drew Claire to him. "But we are going to be married, and our name will be Fremont."

Hilda Beck's eyes misted. The champagne had

218

given her face a rosy glow. "I think it's absolutely splendid about the two of you. I knew things would sort themselves out in time. Avery asked me to convey his congratulations."

"How is he?" Luke asked.

"Much better now. He is selling the Hôtel and, as soon as the legal problems connected with the orderly's death are resolved, we intend to find another line of work." Her face grew quite pink. "Chang, I have a confession to make. Remember the fire in the kitchen annex the night after Avery was shot at? Well, I—I set the fire."

"You!" Chang exploded.

"Yes. Avery was so upset. I was sure it was connected with Mr. Dorn, something out of the past. I thought that what seemed to be another attempt on his life would compel him to reveal the secret. And it worked." She turned to Claire. "But I didn't realize that there would be so much awful publicity about your son. I'm sorry, my dear. All that speculation that your son might still be alive."

"But Christopher is—" Sara began.

"Sara, for God's sake!" Bob roared.

Her face crumpled, and she looked at Claire in mute apology.

Luke felt Claire tremble. They had agreed that, except for Chang, and Sara and Bob, no one must know that Christopher was alive. They intended to contact a famous professor at Cornell University whose book *Dragons of Eden*, which traced the evolution of man, seemed to indicate that he might be able to interpret Dr. Vasa's taped information.

Puzzled, Hilda Beck looked at the crushed Sara and the angry Bob. In that moment, decision came to Chang.

He stood and looked around the room, aware that the scene, his Western friends and the plethora of green and brightly colored foliage, would live in his memory forever. He said slowly, "I have an announcement to make. I am taking a trip to see my family. In Hong Kong and China."

His announcement not only diverted the conversation, it electrified it. Everyone asked questions at once.

He held up his hands. "No, no. There's nothing sudden about it. I have been contemplating a trip for a long time. And I think Jade will go with me."

Jade nodded. "I am nurse now at home. But not here in the English language. It is hard to remember and so easy to forget."

Everyone laughed, but not unkindly. Hilda Beck, surprisingly enough, pointed out that Jade had transposed the words of a famous popular song.

Only Luke frowned. Chang had not been thinking of going to China. He had been so proud of his greenhouse and his work as a police officer. But particularly proud of the years he had sponsored members of his family in America. "When are you leaving?"

"As soon as it can be arranged."

"So soon! Why?"

Chang said slowly, avoiding Luke's glance. "Perhaps I am beginning another journey. That reminds me, I have some things to see to in the greenhouse. If the ladies agree, perhaps we could have dinner shortly. I won't be long." He left the room.

"There's just one more thing," Sara said aggressively. "Did you ever think how strange life is? What happened began and ended in the same place. In Silverleaf. Christopher was born there and you found. . ." she gulped. "I mean, you and Luke fell in love there. . .I have a super idea. Let's all go to Silverleaf. We can have a picnic in the swamp and eat those enormous strawberries. But Claire, don't get pregnant before we go."

Claire laughed. "I forgot to tell you. Chang found

the exact spot where we had the picnic. He took cuttings of the strawberry vines. It is so large because of an akaloid. . .I forget the name. . .which doubles the cells if the plant is watered with a solution at the proper time. What is the akaloid called, Luke?''

"Colchicine." He stared blankly. "My God!"

He ran from the room and went directly to the greenhouse. Chang was there, taping two cardboard cartons which had been punctured with air holes at regular intervals. When he saw Luke, he sat back on his heels. There was a lengthy silence between the two men.

Finally Luke said, "You aren't coming back. You intend to stay in China."

"Yes."

"Chang, I can't let you do this."

Chang said sadly, "My friend, there is no way you can prevent it. How did you guess?"

"When Sara began talking about the picnic. And the strawberries they ate when Claire was pregnant. I won't let you go! The vines are in the boxes, aren't they?"

"Yes. But it is already too late. Dr. Vasa's tapes and an explanatory letter are on a plane, addressed to a cousin in Hong Kong. I promised that one day I would tell you about Laotse's Tao. The voice of Tao, *ye, hei, wei,* is invisible, inaudible and intangible. It eludes inquiry but it blends and becomes One. When I explored the swamp, Tao guided me to the area where the foliage was enormously enlarged. An ancient subterranean source of colchicine, perhaps masses of crocuses that had bloomed, died and stratified before human life began, was nourishing the foliage in that area. At the time, I thought that Tao had given me a source of financial support. I could cultivate the fruit.''

"The colchicine was in the strawberries and Claire ate them?"

Chang nodded. "Yes. That was the secret that Tao wished to impart. At the precise moment, as with my plants, when the seedling begins its long struggle for maturity, Claire ate the strawberries. The foetus was approximately six months old, when the quickening in a woman's womb begins. When the foetus proves its existence and asserts its will to live."

Luke watched helplessly while Chang finished taping the second box. "Do you realize what this means? If Vasa was right, a superior race of human beings will develop. But what will happen then? Will life improve or does it threaten all of us? Chang, you can't risk it."

"There will be many mistakes made. But would this secret be any safer in your people's hands? What would Jasper Dorn have done with it?"

"Everything should be destroyed. Forgotten!"

"And oppose the will of Tao. It can't be done. It is impossible. Listen, Luke. You know all that I know. Christopher is alive, somewhere in your vast country. You have the means and the technological processes at your command. You will spend many years exploring this knowledge. And so will we. Many pregnancies will fail to respond before one will succeed. But the evolution is inevitable."

"Chang, I never knew you, at all. I can't believe you would do this. What can you possibly hope to achieve?"

"What all men want, regardless of the color of their skin or the sounds of their language. What Jasper Dorn lived, and possibly died, to protect. Esteem, honor, a position of affluence and power. For me, being the means through whom Tao chose to communicate is reward enough. But for my family, there will be education, wealth and position for centuries to come. That is my reward, too."

"Luke, are you out there?" It was Claire. She stood

in the doorway. "You missed the late news. There wasn't too much about us. A more important story broke. Survival Kit. It's predicted that it will pass both Houses. But the controversy over it will be bitter." Both men were so silent, she looked at them, frowning. "What were you talking about?"

Chang said in a low voice, "Survival."

Claire touched Luke's arm. "Is something wrong?"

"Nothing that the future won't solve," Luke said. "I hope."

"Well, come along," she said. "Dinner's almost ready."

Chang walked with Claire. Luke followed more slowly, recalling his recent words. . .there are no secrets between Claire and me. What would he do with this amazing and terrifying knowledge? Luke stood on the threshold of mature perception. Like the earthly weight Atlas carried forever on his shoulders, there was an intolerable burden inherent in esteem, honor and a position of affluence and power. An invisible demarcation between personal and professional integrity, between honesty and dishonesty, between sanity and insanity.

There would be no easy solution.

Epilogue

Los Angeles *Times,* September 15.

Anthony Kelsonovitch, known as Kelso, member of a commune near Belden Beach, California, was arrested yesterday and charged with the murder of Jasper Dorn, industrialist and financier, whose body was found on the grounds of an exclusive nursing home, Hôtel del Sol, in Belden Beach, ten days ago. Kelso was taken into custody in South Los Angeles while pawning an expensive watch belonging to Mr. Dorn. Sheriff Marc Mintner of Monterey County stated that police had been looking for Kelso on a charge of willful destruction of private property, a greenhouse belonging to Deputy John Chang, also of Belden Beach. Kelso insisted that the mugging and death had taken place in an isolated cove near the Costa Marina where he had accidentally come across Mr. Dorn sitting alone in a rented car. In an attempt to prevent identification, Kelso had mutilated Mr. Dorn's face and had taken his wallet and personal belongings, overlooking an itinerary of Mr. Dorn's recent trip to Washington, D.C. Kelso insisted that he had not transported the body to the grounds of the nursing home and that he had no idea why it had been found there. Mr. Dorn's immediate family, Mr. Luke Fremont and Mrs. Claire Dorn, were informed of the arrest but could not be reached for comment.

A delay in Kelso's trial is expected as he is undergoing psychiatric examination of hallucinatory episodes during which he confuses Mr. Dorn with an unknown member of the commune who was subjected to torture and forcible restraint.

Federal authorities in charge of the investigation stated that local police had been exceptionally cooperative and they are satisfied that the case has been successfully concluded.